KEPT BY SEDUCTION

Also by Jaymie Holland

Taken by Passion
Claimed by Pleasure
Bound by Desire

KEPT BY SEDUCTION

Jaymie Holland

St. Martin's Griffin
New York

This is a work of fiction. All of the characters, organizations, and events portrayed in this novel are either products of the author's imagination or are used fictitiously.

 Printed in the United States of America. For information, address St. Martin's Press, 175 Fifth Avenue, New York, N.Y. 10010.

www.stmartins.com

Design by Anna Gorovoy

ISBN 978-0-312-38664-1

First published in the United States in e-book format under the title Wonderland: *King of Clubs* by Ellora's Cave Publishing, Inc.

First St. Martin's Griffin Edition: August 2012

10 9 8 7 6 5 4 3 2 1

To:

Puawai Ashley, Karen Morris, Johanna Durling, Devilish Dot,
& all the fabulous ladies of Chey's Fantasies group
for all of your support and enthusiasm.

And to Sire Don
for helping me outfit Ty & Awai's dungeon. ;-)

AUTHOR'S NOTE

DEAR READER,

The "Wonderland" series comes to a fantastical conclusion in *Kept by Seduction,* the fourth book in the four-book series originally published with an e-publisher as Wonderland: *King of Clubs* by Cheyenne McCray. It is published in its entirety.

This award-winning, bestselling romantic erotica "Wonderland" series is being republished under the name Jaymie Holland to clearly distinguish it from other works by me. I believe it is important that my readers know when they read this series that it is extreme in nature from other books by me they may have read before.

Kept by Seduction, as Wonderland: *King of Clubs,* was given amazing reviews including a 4½ star TOP PICK review from the *RT Book Reviews* magazine.

Author's Note

I hope you enjoy *Kept by Seduction* and your journey to a world where not everything is as it seems.

Cheyenne McCray
aka Jaymie Holland

KEPT BY SEDUCTION

PROLOGUE

King Ty raked his fingers through his white-blond hair as he surveyed his lands from a hilltop behind the palace. Cherry blossoms bloomed in abundance, a snowy drift tumbling down the side of the mountain. The air smelled fresh and clean, of spring and sweet blossoms.

The Kingdom of Clubs thrived despite the mental plague holding all of Tarok hostage. Ty's subjects were in good health and good spirits, and hopeful the curse would soon be broken.

Now that Mikaela was believed to be dead.

Even though she had cursed them with her mindspells, and had attempted to harm his brothers' mates, Ty's heart still ached for the sister he had grown up with and loved. He couldn't help but wonder what had happened to the young woman who had once been filled with life and love—beyond the obvious pain of being excluded when their parents divided the Kingdom of Tarok between their four sons. Why the former High King and Queen had excluded Mikaela, the four brothers would never know. Their parents had died shortly after, leaving no explanations.

Devastated, Mikaela had begun to change from the sparkling sister who had made her four brothers laugh and drove them to distraction. She seemed to age, to grow sallow, irritable, and unapproachable. And then, without warning or discussion, Mikaela had wed Balin, the King of Malachad. Malachad, a smaller kingdom to the south, had always been an oath-enemy of Tarok.

Of all the kings Mikaela could have chosen . . . But what was done was done.

And for the past two decades, all of Tarok had suffered the consequences.

Amongst all four kingdoms, there had been no births for over two decades. But Ty's brothers—Jarronn, Darronn, and Karn—had found their mates, and for the first time in these many years, babes had been born into the Kingdoms of Hearts, Spades, and Diamonds.

Now it was Ty's turn to find his mate.

His lips curved into a rogue's smile as he sought to picture his future queen. Unlike his brothers, who were initially reluctant to take on a mate from another world, Ty relished the opportunity. He had tired of the women in his court and, if truth be told, he had enjoyed watching his brothers tame their mates . . . or in some cases be somewhat tamed themselves.

At the thought of his sister-in-joining, Alexi, Ty reflexively covered his ballocks with his hand. Indeed, she was not a woman to cross.

A late spring wind brushed Ty's hair across his back as he watched a pregnant *anlia* doe nibbling at the feathered blue leaves of a *ch'tok* tree. The female deer ate from the *ch'tok* only when they carried their young, providing special nutrients to their unborn babes.

"Majesty." Kalina's musical voice summoned his attention and he turned to look at the black-haired, amber-eyed sorceress. Her black robes clung to her curvaceous shape, the wind molding the material to her body. Her nipples pressed against the cloth and he could see the outline at the juncture of her thighs. Ty's cock stirred and he imagined taking the sorceress again and again. He had often shared pleasures with Kalina over the many years he had known her.

She gave him an alluring smile. "I am ready for you now."

He nodded to the loyal sorceress. "I will join you shortly."

"Yes, Majesty." Kalina bowed. The club charm at her collar dangled against her throat as she rose from her bow.

Ty watched her walk away, her bare feet silent against the soft grass as she returned to the palace. She disappeared behind the open walls that blended in with the greens of the hillside like moss on trees.

His blood heated as he imagined what his future mate might look like and he flexed his muscles at the thought of finally choosing. He headed to the palace with a sense of purpose to his stride.

He entered his palace, his boot steps echoing down the hallway. Sunshine spilled into the palace from countless windows, making it bright and airy, unlike his brother Karn's dark and gloomy mansion. Although, since Annie had become the Queen of Diamonds, Diamond Hall seemed far less foreboding. Her presence had brought love, light, and joy to Karn's life and to the lives of his subjects.

Ty strode down the wide hallway, and when he entered Kalina's candlelit chambers, he found the sorceress in the embrace of Kir, lord of Emerald City and of the mountain-wolf clan. Kir was Ty's comrade, almost like a brother, and the two oft shared women, including the sorceress. Kalina's robe was open, her lush breasts exposed and Kir was tugging at the club charms dangling from her pierced nipples. He was kissing her in a long, slow kiss that Ty knew Kalina enjoyed.

"Kir," Ty said to the bare-chested man as he moved to the sorceress's *a'bin*. "I see you have returned to sample my beauty's treasures."

Kalina laughed softly and Kir gave a wolfish growl. "I hope to convince this lovely lady to join my pack when she has completed her duties with you."

"But I am a weretiger," she said as she cupped Kir's erection through his leather breeches. "Why would I want to join with a pack of werewolves?"

Kir slipped one hand down her belly to her mons, and slid one finger into her folds, causing her to gasp. "You would have a home with my people, always," he said. "You would never be passed from one man to the next like a belonging. You would have the choice to bed any man you wish to, and to mate for life if you choose."

A look passed across Kalina's features, perhaps one of longing and regret, but it was quickly replaced by an expression of ecstasy as Kir began suckling one of her nipples, his tongue circling the nipple charm.

Ty's cock hardened at the sight of the two lovers as he held his hand high above the single remaining card on the *a'bin.* The card glowed and vibrated against the flat surface. "Kir is right, Kalina," Ty said as he reached for the card. "When your duties here have been satisfied, you may leave." The card jumped into his hand as he turned back to the sorceress and added, "But know you will always have a home in my kingdom."

"Thank you, Majesty." Kalina's voice was breathless as she worked at the fastenings on Kir's breeches.

Ty flipped the card over. His cock bucked against his breeches and a rumbling purr rose in his throat at the sight of the lovely woman who was to be his queen. She was beautiful with dark chestnut brown hair and eyes as blue as the feathery leaves of the *ch'tok* trees. Even though she had the bearing of a warrior woman, Ty sensed her heart was scarred and her eyes held a hint of old wounds.

Awai, the name came to him like a whisper on the wind, and it sounded like *ah-why. Yes, her name is Awai.*

The sounds of lovemaking met Ty's ears and he turned to see Kir flat on his back, still wearing his breeches, and Kalina riding his cock.

Ty felt the need for release, so intense was his desire for his future queen. He strode to where the couple were fucking, knelt behind Kalina, and unfastened his breeches. With his magic he summoned a handful of sandalwood-scented gel and coated his cock with it before sliding into Kalina's tight ass.

She moaned as he and Kir fucked her and Ty couldn't help but imagine it was his future queen that he was thrusting into. He gripped Kalina's hip with one hand and held up the card with his other so that he could watch Awai's face.

Yes, he would more than enjoy sliding into her hot core and driving her to orgasm.

Would she accept domination readily, like Jarronn's Alice? With hesitance and warmth, like Annie of Diamonds? Or would she require compromise, like Darronn's ever-fiery Alexi?

Kalina's body quaked with her orgasm and she gave gasping sobs of pleasure with each jolt of her body. Kir growled and thrust up hard, and Ty knew the werewolf had spilled his seed into the sorceress.

Ty continued pumping in and out of Kalina's ass, the image of Awai growing stronger and stronger until he was almost positive it was her he was fucking. With a tiger's roar, Ty came like he had never climaxed before.

The face on the card never left his mind, in that moment, or the moments that followed.

Ready, hesitant, fiery, or anything in between, Ty was prepared for his mate. He felt confident he could win her, hopeful that he could love her—and now, he felt driven to heal the pain he had seen in her eyes.

"I am coming, my sweet," he growled, still feeling the heat of his fantasy. "Be prepared."

CHAPTER ONE

AWAI STEELE PACED THE LENGTH OF HER CONdominium, her heels sinking into the deep, lush burgundy carpeting. She preferred not to wear a bra when she wasn't working, and the silky material of her blouse rasped her nipples, making them taut with hunger. Her short skirt brushed her upper thighs and the falling star at her belly button swung against her flat belly.

The condo smelled of carpet shampoo, pine cleaner, and fresh paint. It was bare of all furnishings, everything put into long-term storage.

Because tonight *they* would come for her.

Awai wrapped her fingers tighter around the handle of her leather whip and snapped the long strip of leather, the crack loud and satisfying. It was exactly a year since Annie vanished, two years for Alexi, and three years to the day since Alice had disappeared.

Without a doubt Awai knew she was next.

"Let them come," she murmured, and snapped her whip again. She didn't know who had taken her nieces, but whoever they were, they would pay dearly if the girls had come to any harm.

After Annie and her cat Abracadabra had vanished, Awai had spent the year preparing for today. The first thing she did was put all of Annie's belongings into storage with Alexi's and Alice's possessions. Then, gradually, throughout the year Awai sold her advertising agency along with all her shares of stock, her condo, and her Mercedes SL600. Every penny Awai owned, totaling well over five million dollars, was in an account earmarked for a women's shelter that aided victims of domestic violence. If Awai didn't return within a specified amount of time, the funds would go to the shelter. Her estate and her nieces' belongings would be taken out of storage and given to the same facility.

Awai paused in her pacing and moved to the expansive window that stretched along two sides of the large common room. Her view of San Francisco was magnificent, and tonight was no exception. City lights glittered in the darkness and so did the lights along the Golden Gate Bridge. No doubt she would miss this view, wherever she was going, but she missed her nieces more. A constant ache had taken residence in her heart and soul, and she wouldn't rest until she found Annie, Alice, and Alexi.

Awai was only a few years older than her nieces, being their aunt by marriage. Long ago she had married the girls' distant uncle, John Steele—

—And the bastard had nearly killed her.

A hard and cold knot expanded in Awai's gut, as it did every time she thought of the son of a bitch. She had been young, innocent, and fresh out of high school when she met John. He had wooed her with his charm and expensive gifts, and had seduced her into his bed.

Awai ran the leather strap of her whip over her palm as her thoughts turned back to that horrid time and her triumph in making a new life for herself.

Once she escaped the bastard, she'd promised herself that no man would ever dominate her again.

Awai raised her chin, no longer seeing the city lights, but instead seeing the light of her past. With her intelligence and drive, Awai had quickly worked her way to the top of her profession in the advertising business. Eventually she had started her own firm, and it wasn't long before she was drawing in larger and larger accounts until her agency was one of the premier advertising firms in the state of California. She became known as a ball buster, the woman with brass ovaries. She didn't take shit from any man, and her staff was populated almost exclusively with women.

She had also started an extensive training program in the domestic violence shelter. With Awai's financial backing, the center taught women the skills necessary to enter the workforce. Frequently, Awai hired women from the shelter in positions such as receptionist or filing clerk. Gradually, as they learned the ropes, many of the women were trained in more demanding tasks and worked their way up through the advertising agency.

Awai shifted and lightly flicked her whip, allowing it

to curl like a sensuous caress around her bare legs and the leather straps from her heels that wrapped around her ankles and calves.

There was another side to her life that no one knew about outside of her niece Annie. Almost every evening, Awai left her daily concerns and entered the world of BDSM as a Dominatrix, Mistress Awai.

Awai treated her submissives well, making sure they enjoyed the erotic play, and always keeping the relationships safe, sane, and consensual. She had chosen to become a Domme simply because she had made that promise to herself . . . that no man would be her master.

Yet something was missing. She couldn't quite place her finger on it, but she didn't feel complete being a Domme. Awai knew what she wanted in life and went after it with a vengeance. So why was her role as a Domme not entirely satisfying?

As if I wished to be the one tied up and at a male Dom's mercy.

She shrugged away the errant thought. *What the hell's the matter with me?*

Awai moved away from the window, a sense of melancholy rolling over her. She was known as a take-charge dynamo, and these feelings of confusion were pissing her off. Yet, as she thought more and more about being a Domme, and of her missing nieces, she felt both angry and brooding . . . and regretful.

Awai snapped her whip in the empty room, the crack of leather jarring her back into her role. She would take charge and let the bastards who stole her nieces know who was boss.

When will they get here? she wondered as she stared at the front door. It was well after ten—only two hours left until midnight and then the anniversary of all her nieces' disappearances would have passed.

Awai frowned at the stately mahogany door. *Could I have been wrong?*

No. She wouldn't allow doubt to make her insecure. Everything in her gut told her that they would be coming for her, too.

Since there wasn't any furniture left in the condo, Awai moved to the wall beside the door. She slid down the wall until she was sitting on the plush burgundy carpeting and set her whip beside her. Awai's short skirt was hiked up to her waist and her thong was pulled tight against her clit. It had been days since she'd had a fuck, and for some reason the last one hadn't been as fulfilling as she'd hoped.

A wild fantasy had gone through her mind as she'd had sex with her sub. A fantasy of riding a powerful man, his cock filling her pussy while another man slid his erection into her ass. And yet a third grabbing her by her hair and forcing her to suck his cock. She was totally at their mercy while all three men fucked her.

At the memory of the fantasy, Awai couldn't help but slide one hand down to her pussy. As she visualized the scene again, she moved aside the thong and fingered her clit. With her free hand she pushed her blouse above her pert breasts, exposing her nipples to the cool air in the condo.

She started out with small circles around her clit, then thrust one finger into her pussy, then spread her juices over her folds. Against her will, she found herself back in the fantasy of the three men. This time one of the men was eating her pussy while another one kissed her, and the third sucked her nipples.

The thought of three gorgeous men focused on her pleasure, and in turn her pleasuring them, sent Awai into orbit. Her orgasm came hard and fast, and caused her to moan as ripple after ripple of her climax continued to flow through her until she came a second time.

After she slipped her hand from her thong and arranged her clothing a bit, Awai relaxed against the wall and closed her eyes. She brought her fingers to her nose and scented herself, wondering what it would be like to smell the come of three men all at once.

What's the matter with me? Why am I fantasizing about dominant men? I should think instead of the men I dominate.

But the men continued to haunt her. Awai sighed and sank further into her thoughts until she slipped into a deep but unsettling sleep.

A blond god of a man tied Awai's wrists together with a glittering golden rope. It was snug, yet the rope didn't hurt or cut into her flesh. In a sensuous caress, he slid his hands down her thighs and calves, then bound her ankles together, too, with another piece of the golden rope. When he finished, he lowered his head to the juncture of her thighs and inhaled deeply, his long blond hair ca-

ressing her skin. He gave a satisfied purr, like a tiger, and she felt a tingle in her pussy and her panties grew wet.

Awai jerked awake and found herself still positioned with her back to the wall of her condo. She blinked, feeling oddly disoriented and almost as if she'd been drugged.

Golden light shone across the living room carpet, yet through the windows in front of her she could still see San Francisco's sparkling nighttime view. Slowly she turned her head and saw that the door was open—

Sunlight was spilling into her home. Not a hall light or a streetlight. It was pure butter yellow sunshine like it shone on a cool spring morning in places where there wasn't any fog to dim it.

Her heart pounded like mad. She tried to get to her feet, only to slide down the wall and fall onto her side, her cheek resting on the leather handle of her whip.

Her hands and ankles were bound, just like in her dream.

Awai's breathing was hard and fast as she glanced at the golden rope around her wrists and then looked to her ankles.

A shadow fell across the carpet.

Awai's gaze shot to the doorway and she saw the golden god from her dreams. The man's white-blond hair tumbled over his shoulders and a gold earring glittered in one ear. His muscled chest was bare, and the tattoo of a club was on his magnificent six-pack abs. Good lord, but those leather pants cradled his impressive family jewels, and despite the fact that she was tied up and at his mercy, Awai's pussy tingled.

Instead of the diatribe she had planned when "they" finally showed up to kidnap her, Awai found herself absolutely speechless.

The golden god flexed his muscles as he moved closer, then knelt before her on one knee. His intense blue eyes focused on her and he smelled of sun-warmed flesh and mountain air. Gently he brushed the back of his hand over her cheek, and in a voice that sent shivers down her spine, the god said, "I have come for you."

CHAPTER TWO

King Ty knelt on one knee and brushed the back of his hand over the woman's cheek as she lay on her side, bound with his golden ropes. How beautiful the woman was, more beautiful than her picture on the card he had taken from the *a'bin*. Even more beautiful than the image he held in his mind as he'd fucked the sorceress.

Awai, he reminded himself. This beauty's name was Awai.

Strands of Awai's chestnut hair framed her face while the rest of her tresses were piled on her head in a style he found sexy and alluring. Her eyes were indeed blue, bluer than his own. And her body . . . perfection with pert breasts showing through her blouse, and prominent nipples made to suck. He continued to stroke her cheek as his gaze traveled lower and he smiled. The woman had lovely thighs to slide between.

Awai's eyes narrowed and glittered with sudden fire.

In a movement that was fast and unexpected, she jerked her mouth toward his hand and buried her teeth in his index finger. Sharp pain shot through his hand as her teeth sank through his flesh down to his bone.

Ty held his ground and didn't flinch. "Not a kitten, but a tigress." He sighed, then gave a quick grin despite the ache in his hand. "After meeting and suffering the temper of Alexi, I should have been better prepared."

Confusion, then anger crossed Awai's features and she released her hold on his finger.

Ty brushed the blood on his hand onto his breeches as Awai glared at him. "If you've hurt Alexi or any of my nieces," she said with more than vengeance in her voice, "I'll kill you."

Chuckling at the memory of that first encounter with Alexi, Ty shook his head. At least he could laugh about it now. "You should have no fear for your kin, tigress. Alexi is well able to care for herself. The day I met her—well, let us just say I could not walk straight for several days."

"Good." Awai was tempted to laugh, but she maintained her angry expression. Here she was, lying on her side, tied up, and yet despite herself she was completely intrigued by this blond god. He reminded her of a rogue or even a rake from a historical romance novel.

Except he had her trussed up like a sacrificial calf at a pagan altar.

"Untie me," she demanded with all the fury she could muster as she struggled to pull apart the bonds at her wrists. "Let me go, damn it."

Still on one knee, the man grabbed Awai by the shoulders and raised her so that she was sitting up, her bound wrists in her lap. Heat from his palms burned through her thin blouse and her breath caught in her chest.

"I am Ty, ruler of the Kingdom of Clubs," he said in a solemn voice. "I have come to take you to my world."

Despite her curiosity and her natural inclination toward disbelief, Awai growled at him, "I don't care if you're the King of Crap. Let me go and take me to my nieces."

The man who called himself Ty chuckled at her words. "I will release your bonds. All I ask is that you trust me—and avoid crippling me in the same manner your niece selected."

Awai's body trembled with anger while Ty waved his hand and the golden ropes at her ankles and wrists simply disappeared. With slow, firm strokes, he massaged her ankles. For a moment Awai allowed herself to feel amazement at his little feat of illusion.

But when Ty started to reach for her now unbound wrists, Awai laced her fingers together and swung her hands up, straight toward his face. In a lightning fast movement, he caught her wrists in one of his large hands, just short of his jaw.

Ty grinned as he released his hold on her. "My little tigress."

I'll show him a tigress.

Awai let loose with all of her frustration and anger at her nieces' disappearances. She fought against his hold with everything she had. As she lashed out at him, she bit her tongue. Her mouth filled with the taste of blood, which only made her more angry.

Ty couldn't believe his stupidity at releasing Awai. He should have simply flung her over his shoulder and brought her through the path and into his world.

"Damnation, woman!" He managed to grab both of Awai's wrists and pin them to the carpet above her head. She continued to struggle, but he straddled her thighs and put just enough weight on her legs to keep her from moving.

Awai's face was red, her blue eyes feral like the tigress she was. He kept her wrists pinned with one hand and the urge to kiss her came over him, to brush his lips over her forehead, to breathe in her musky perfume. He wanted to relieve her fears, to soothe her fury.

Ty's face neared Awai's and her eyes suddenly blurred. Images flooded her mind . . . of being trapped by her ex-husband, his breath hot and smelling of alcohol. Of being helpless beneath him.

"No!" Awai let loose with a scream and fought even harder to free herself, but she was held entirely immobile. Fear replaced the anger, and tears fogged her vision as she struggled. She wouldn't let him hurt her again. Never again!

From a distance she heard a male voice speaking to her with a gentleness she'd never heard from a man before. "I am sorry, Awai." His tone was full of regret. "I shouldn't have tried to kiss you. Please forgive me."

Slowly her vision cleared and instead of the foul beast

who had brutalized her, she saw the golden god. He still held her wrists above her head with one hand and with his other he carefully brushed tears from her eyes. She was breathing hard, and her muscles were aching as though she'd raced a marathon. Gradually her body relaxed.

Damn, she hadn't cried for years . . . since she'd escaped John Steele and made a new life for herself. Her breath continued to come in harsh gulps and her heart pounded in her throat. Her body was covered in sweat. How could she have lost her sanity so completely in that one moment?

"The path will soon close, my tigress." Ty trailed his thumb across her lips and gave her a soft smile. "If we do not leave now we will be trapped in this world and it will be another year of your time before you see your loved ones, or I see my people."

Awai cleared her throat. "Oh."

Ty's gaze held hers. "Will you come with me if I release you?"

This was what she had prepared for all year long, and she was fighting it like a crazy woman.

She bit the inside of her lip, then nodded. "I'll go with you as long as you promise that I'll see my family."

Ty released his hold on her and scooped up her leather whip as he stood. "You have my word." He held out his free hand. "Come. The path is closing."

Awai was still shaking as she took his hand. The sunshine that had spilled through her doorway before was now murky, as if shrouded by thunderclouds. Ty pulled her toward the dull light at a jog, and she had no choice but to follow him. Her heart pounded with both fear and hope.

They dove into the gloom and Awai felt like she was tumbling through thick paste. Sticky and gooey, like the fat pots of glue she'd used in kindergarten all those years ago. The sensation clung to her face and hands, her bare belly and legs.

And then they were free of the goo—falling into bright sunshine and a brilliant green world. Ty caught her to him as he landed with a *whump.* He rolled onto his back in a bed of soft grass, Awai cradled close to his chest. She found herself face-to-face, chest-to-chest . . . erect cock to mound.

Heat flushed her face as she stared down at her would-be kidnapper. The gooey feeling from the path or whatever it was had vanished, and she now felt only light wind caressing her cheeks and Ty between her legs. His leather pants felt as soft as butter against the skin of her thighs, and her thong pulled against her clit in a manner that made her crazy with need.

"Now this is the position I prefer," she said with a little smile that came out of nowhere.

Ty laughed, and in a quick movement he turned so that Awai was on her side in the grass, her leg hooked over his thigh. They were still face-to-face. Her eyes were wide, but this time he didn't see anger or fear in their blue depths.

"For now, let us start on equal footing." Ty said, smiling at the surprise in her expression. "But know that I am your king, and soon you will desire to submit to me in every way."

"I have no king." She shook her head, grass brushing her cheek and her lips. "I'm a Domme. Men submit to me."

He laughed again and ran a finger down her pert nose. "You will see, my little tigress."

Awai pushed herself up on one elbow so that she was looking down at Ty. He was gorgeous and purely male. She didn't even know him and she wanted him like no man she'd ever met before. A man who could fulfill her secret fantasies that she'd never shared with anyone . . .

If she admitted how much she wanted to make them come true, could she forget her past and allow herself to be controlled by a man?

She spotted her whip lying on the grass beside Ty, grabbed it by the handle, and got to her feet. Awai was tempted to show the man how well she knew how to use it, but she only practiced safe, sane, and consensual BDSM. No doubt this man wouldn't consent to being whipped. He was a Dom through and through.

In a slow demonstration of masculine ease, the golden god got to his feet. Lord, but his muscles rippled and flexed with power. Awai's nipples tightened and her pussy grew wetter. He was bigger, buffer, and probably the most well-hung man she'd ever had the pleasure of meeting, if the size of the package behind his leather pants was any indication. Every sensible thought since meeting Ty had vanished and all she knew was that she wanted him.

Damn.

With every muscular movement he made, she knew he could crush her if he wanted, could hurt her in so many ways. Why then did she feel safe with him? Just because he hadn't hurt her in her home?

But when he moved toward her, she stiffened, suddenly remembering that she'd been kidnapped into this world, as no doubt Annie, Alexi, and Alice had been.

Well, Awai thought, *actually I came willingly to find my nieces. They might have been kidnapped, but I wasn't.*

Ty held out his hand to Awai and hoped she would trust him. After a moment of indecision in her blue eyes, she took it. Her fingers felt small and cool in his palm and he could sense the tenseness radiating through her body.

"Let me show you my realm," he said as he led her away from where they'd landed in the grass. He was proud of his lands and his people, and he hoped that she would be pleased with what she saw.

Awai had been so intent on the man that she hadn't even noticed her surroundings. She stared in wonder as sunlight shone down through blue-green clouds and spilled onto trees with feathery blue leaves, others with lacey green leaves, and yet others with colorful flowers. Ahead of them a waterfall of white blooms flowed down the hillside. If she wasn't mistaken, they were cherry blossoms.

Countless flowers in unusual shapes dotted the grassy hillside in bursts of orange, pink, red, blue, and purple. Their sweet perfume mingled with the earthy smell of the land and the warm scent of the man beside her. Their footsteps were silent as they walked down the grassy hill.

In the distance she could see a small town or a village with people and industry. Nearer to them she saw a sprawling building that reminded her of an Egyptian palace, even though the walls were a green-beige color. It was as if the building were camouflaged to blend in with the surrounding trees, flowers, and the grassy hillside.

Ty squeezed her hand, bringing her back to the present. She looked up at him and he smiled, a cute boyish smile that made her heart melt. Damn, she was supposed to be kicking ass and taking names. Instead she was lusting over this man like a besotted schoolgirl with a crush on the captain of the football team.

"Ah . . ." Awai cleared her throat and brought them to a stop. She attempted to return to her "I am queen of the universe" presence that she maintained in the corporate world. "Where the hell are Annie, Alexi, and Alice?"

He looked thoughtful for a moment, as if trying to determine how much to tell her. When he spoke, it was in a clear, concise tone. "Alice is joined with my brother Jarronn and she is now the High Queen of Tarok and Queen of Hearts." Awai's jaw dropped, but Ty continued, "Alexi is my brother Darronn's bride, and she is Queen of Spades."

At this point Awai was ready to use the whip she still carried. He had to be lying. But Ty was saying, "Annie has mated with my brother Karn, and she is Queen of Diamonds." He grinned. "Although her cat Abra thinks *she* rules Diamond Hall."

Awai jerked her hand from Ty's and backed away

from him like his derangement was contagious. "You're freaking nuts, aren't you." It wasn't a question—she was positive he was crazy. Well, almost positive. "What are you guys? A deck of cards?"

Ty gave her that boyish grin that made her stomach quiver. "My parents divided the Kingdom of Tarok into four separate kingdoms before they died." He gestured to the lands as though encompassing everything around him. "My mother was a Seer. She loved to play card games, and she chose to name the kingdoms after each of the suites in a deck of playing cards. The Kingdom of Tarok was named after another game she enjoyed."

Awai gestured to his abdomen. "And the tattoo on your stomach?"

He shrugged. "Once the kingdoms were divided, our mother insisted on tattooing each of us. She was an artist, much like your Annie."

Without consciously realizing it, Awai moved closer to Ty, concern clenching her heart. "She's all right, isn't she? Annie was always so much gentler than Alice, and especially Alexi, and she could be hurt so easily. Please tell me she's happy here."

This time Ty's look was serious as he nodded and took Awai by the shoulders. "Annie is truly a blessing to Tarok, and especially the Kingdom of Diamonds. She is dearly loved by all, as are Alexi and Alice."

Awai wanted to cry with relief, yet how could she know if Ty was telling the truth?

"I want to kiss you," Ty said in a deep, husky voice that made her shiver. "May I?"

The fact that he asked her, that he recognized her fear of being taken against her will, melted Awai's heart even further. She placed her palms on his smooth yet rock-hard chest and pressed close to him as she whispered, "Yes."

Ty gave her his rogue's smile that made her want to swoon like a romance novel heroine. She closed her eyes when he lowered his face and lightly brushed his lips over hers. Awai waited for more, but he took the kiss no further.

She opened her eyes and saw only tenderness in his expression. Awai Steele always took what she wanted in life, and right now she wanted a real kiss from this man. She slid her arms up and around his neck and pulled his face down to meet hers.

Awai moved her lips over his and he gently returned her kiss. But as she demanded more of him, his kiss matched hers in intensity. He groaned, sliding his hands from her shoulders and down her arms to her hips where he pressed her tight to his erection. He was so tall and his cock obviously so big that she felt him at her belly button, his hard-on smashing her star charm into her flesh, causing her to feel a sensation of both pain and pleasure.

Ty's tongue thrust into her mouth, demanding, insistent, as if he could no longer rein in his desire for her. Awai gave herself up to the taste of him, to his smell, to the feel of his hard body against hers and the heat of his flesh burning through her clothing. This man would be the kind of lover she had dreamed about in her secret fantasies. The man who could tie her up and do the things to her she had only imagined, or the things she had done to her subs.

With this man, she could be submissive. And she'd be safe.

But how can I know that for certain?

Awai broke the kiss and pulled away from Ty. As his blue eyes looked into hers, that old fear and anger that had been in her heart and soul too long returned to her, thanks to that bastard of an ex-husband.

Could she relinquish control? Could she allow Ty to put her in a position where she was helpless and at his mercy?

CHAPTER THREE

Ty sensed the change in Awai and knew that she struggled against giving herself to him. She wanted him, of that he was certain. He could see it in her expressive blue eyes, could scent her arousal, could see her erect nipples pushing against her clothing.

It was in his nature to dominate and he was used to submissive women. But Awai was different. From the start, when he had first seen her wounded eyes in the magical playing card, he had known she had deep pain to overcome before she would or could fully trust him. The only way he could break through her barriers would be to dominate her completely, to have her turn her trust and faith and control over to him. Only then could she allow herself to have the love her heart desired . . . and the pleasure.

He had no doubt that whether or not Awai would admit it, within her very being she craved domination. He sensed it at the deepest level of his soul.

Before she had the chance to refuse his advances, or

to regret her own, Ty took Awai's hand and gently pulled her down the hill toward his palace. It lay far below, its soft-toned walls glowing in the late spring sunlight.

She allowed him to lead her, but as they walked she asked, "Are my nieces here? I want to see them now."

"They are each in their respective kingdoms." He glanced down at her and saw the frustration and disappointment in her expression. "I will send word that you have arrived."

Ty kept his tone even, hoping she would accept what he had to say next. "Your family members have been expecting you, but it will take them time to prepare for the trip. The kings and queens will need to handle matters in their kingdoms and it will take time to journey here. I am quite certain they will want to bring their children."

Awai came to an abrupt stop, jerking against Ty's hand, bringing him to a stop, too. Her head swam with what he had just said. Shit, how could he just pop that one on her as if it was no big deal?

"Children?" Her voice squeaked as she spoke and she could only stare at him with incredulity.

He smiled, but this time she wanted to slug him. "Between the three queens and kings, they have many cubs," he said.

She blinked. "Cubs?"

But Ty was still talking. "Alice and Jarronn have three sets of twins, Alexi and Darronn have triplet boys and a new daughter, and Annie also has an infant female cub."

Awai released Ty's hand and dropped to the ground

beneath a flowery moss-covered tree. Grass prickled her butt as she buried her face in her hands. Her elbows braced on her knees, she tried to absorb the fact that the girls were now all mothers.

Mothers!

Unless Ty was lying through his teeth.

She raised her head to find that he was now sitting next to her, studying her with a calm expression on his handsome features.

"You're serious, aren't you?" She pushed her dark hair out of her face and glared at him. "My nieces are some kind of baby factories for your world."

At that Ty frowned. "Annie, Alexi, and Alice each love their mates. They chose to join with my brothers and they each chose to bear children."

Awai shook her head, a loose tendril of hair falling back across her face. "Maybe Annie and Alice, but Alexi is too much like me, too career-driven to want to have kids."

Ty's frown deepened. "You do not wish to have offspring?"

"Are you kidding?" Awai raised her hands. "Look at me. I'm in my thirties, I'm set in my ways, and I don't want to have kids that will end up having an old mother when they grow up."

The corner of Ty's mouth quirked. "You are but a youngling compared to the people of my world. I am well over two hundred of your Earth years."

It was all too much. Awai flung herself on her back in

the grass, her arms above her. Her head was really spinning now. She stared up at the tree and at the aqua-colored clouds peeking through the lacey leaves. “I can’t take this,” she muttered.

Ty’s groin tightened as he studied his future queen. When Awai lay back in the grass, her tunic rose up and exposed the plump undersides of her breasts and her skirt hiked to the top of her thighs, almost showing her quim. With her arms above her head, her position was one of complete submission.

She was closer to surrendering herself to him than she realized. Closer than even he had realized.

From the moment he had met Awai, Ty had sensed that her act of dominance over men was simply that—an act.

He reached out with one hand and stroked the undersides of her breasts. Awai audibly caught her breath and her blue gaze turned from the sky to him. Her lips parted, and the scent of her arousal grew stronger. While slowly caressing her, he continued to keep his eyes locked with hers. She visibly swallowed as she arched her back, and her expression told him she could not help her reaction to his touch.

“Ty,” she whispered, even as she was drawn to his touch, “I don’t know if I’m ready for this.”

Lightly he trailed his fingers from her breasts, down her stomach to the silver shooting star at her belly button. He wanted to suckle her nipples then lick the path his hand had taken, but he feared moving too fast would upset her again. “You enjoy the pleasures of men, do you not?” he murmured.

She shivered as his finger circled the star. "Yes . . . but I never have sex with a man who wants to dominate me."

"I will dominate you." His hand continued past the star to the belt that cradled her hips. "With your trust and consent. Only by submitting to me will you truly heal."

After what she'd been through with Ty—whether it had been hours or minutes—it seemed like a lifetime. She'd experienced one emotion after another: anger, fear, terror, hope, attraction, arousal, the desire to submit . . . and a feeling of trust that went soul-deep.

Yes, somehow she trusted him, even though she barely knew him. Hell, she'd just met him.

But she wanted him. Desperately.

At what cost, though?

"It must be your choice to submit to me." Ty's hand stopped at her belly, just before her mound. His face was serious and his tone solemn as his gaze held hers. "But once you make that choice, you must obey my commands without question. The only occasion you may question me is if you are frightened by what I ask of you. That is also the only time you may refuse me."

Crap.

Yet everything in her soul was telling her to take this opportunity and run with it. To give it a shot, to see if she was a submissive inside . . . to see if she really did want to be dominated, but hadn't been able to admit it out loud.

But jeez. She'd barely met the man, she reminded herself yet again. Although that hadn't stopped her before at the BDSM clubs in San Francisco. She'd had the birth-control implant in her arm so that she couldn't get pregnant and had always kept a supply of condoms on hand. At the clubs she had taken what she wanted from men, when she wanted.

But submit to Ty?

Go for it, her inner voice urged. *You'll never know if you don't try.*

Everything about him made her feel special and excited. It didn't make sense how she could feel this way with a man who had something to do with her nieces' disappearances, a man whom she'd just met, a man who had purposely taken her from her own world to his . . . but he had given her the choice. And even more impressive, he would have stayed in her world if she had not come with him.

Ty's blond hair moved in the breeze that stirred grass against her cheeks and caressed her belly. She saw the golden hair on his arm move in the light wind and caught the scent of his male musk. His palm was hot through her skirt where his hand rested just above her mound.

Awai's pussy was wet and her nipples hard and aching beneath her blouse. Her body wanted him, her mind wanted him, and her gut instinct told her he was a good man. And a gorgeous man at that. Blond, blue-eyed, built like a pro bodybuilder. Damn, she could jump him right this moment.

But to be dominated . . .

The ground was as hard as a floor beneath her as she squeezed her eyes tight.

Images of being flat on her back on a hardwood floor

filled her mind. Of John Steele standing over her after he'd knocked her down.

Tears burned at the back of Awai's eyes as she rolled away from Ty and scrambled to her feet. Pain from the memory lanced through her head, but she would not shed one more goddamn tear over that man.

I promised myself. I promised!

Her heels sank into the soft earth and grass as she moved away from Ty. She walked until she was at the highest rise of the hill, overlooking a sweep of white cherry blossoms. She looked down at the rolling terrain from the drop beneath her, to the lake beyond that. She hugged her arms tight to her chest as if that would protect her from the memories of that bastard who had brutalized her until she had finally escaped him.

Ty eased to his feet as he watched Awai walk away. A thousand heart-wounds weighted her soul, so tangible he could feel them in the very air around him.

Damnation. He cursed himself for his stupidity again. For pushing her too hard, too fast. His instincts and senses told him she had much to overcome, yet he had barreled ahead like a *harline* bull in rutting fervor.

Awai stood at the top of the hill with her back to him, rigid with defiance and pain. She was so beautiful, so proud. Ty's soul ached for her, and he wanted to do whatever he could to make her smile again. To heal the wounds and make her happy.

With the silence and grace of his species, Ty moved up to the rise until he was so close he could feel her body heat, could sense her sadness and anger, smell her perfume of orchids and musk. When he grasped her shoulders with his large hands, Awai tensed, then relaxed as he pulled her against his chest. He slipped his hands down her arms and around her bare waist, and settled his chin on the top of her head.

"I am sorry, tigress, I should not have pushed you so soon." He breathed in the scent of her hair, felt her shuddering sigh at his words. "Of all that you see before you, I am the ruler, my sweet. As king I never have had to ask for submission. It is simply a part of our lives, something that my people enjoy."

"I understand." Awai's voice was quiet as she spoke. "I don't like to admit to fear of any kind, but please understand that this is a part of me . . . to fear submitting to a man." She gave a soul-deep sigh then continued, "Long ago I was physically abused and almost killed by my ex-husband. I swore I'd never let any man dominate me again."

Ty stiffened at her words, rage overcoming him like a thunderstorm. How dare any man abuse a woman? And this woman, his tigress . . . "I will kill the bastard if he still lives," he growled out, his words nearly a roar. "Once a path opens, you will lead me to him and I will see that he never harms another woman again."

Awai couldn't believe the vehemence in Ty's statement. She turned around in his embrace, placed her palms flat against his bare chest, and tilted her head up to look at him. "John isn't worth it. I decided long ago that I wouldn't waste any time or energy on that man again."

"But look what he has done to you." Ty pressed her closer to him, his hands now at her lower back. "You fear what you desire most. He still rules your future because of his cruelty in your past. To move forward you *must* meet head-on your greatest fears."

"Maybe that promise I made to myself, to not be controlled by any man, has lost its usefulness." She smiled, the corners of her mouth trembling. "I think that maybe it even gives power to my ex." She gave a soul-shuddering sigh and shook her head. "But I need time . . . time to let it all go."

Ty narrowed his brows as he gave another feral growl. "Once you are healed, once you have all that you desire, I will take care of the bastard."

Awai shivered at the intensity of Ty's growl. "How do you do that growling thing? You don't sound like a man . . . you sound like a lion, or a tiger."

He stepped back, his hands slipping away from her waist, the warmth of his chest gone and leaving her cold. "Better now than later," he said, his expression gentle.

Awai's head buzzed and she felt as if she'd slipped right into an episode of an old werewolf movie as she stared at Ty—or what had been Ty. He was shifting, his mouth elongating into a muzzle, white and black hair covering his skin, a tail growing from his ass, and his arms turning into legs as he lowered to the ground and crouched on all fours. Whiskers sprouted from his face, and he gave a low roar.

She brought her hand to her chest. "You're a tiger."

Weretiger, he corrected in her mind.

Awai stumbled back. "You talked—in my head!" Never mind that she was now speaking with a freaking tiger.

When in weretiger form, we have the ability to thought-speak. He eased toward her, like a predator stalking its prey, and she took another step back. Ty stopped. *Do not move, Awai,* he said, his tone urgent.

Before Awai could ask what he meant, one of her high heels slipped. She was too shocked to scream as her whole body dropped to the ground. In the next second she started to slide down the hillside.

In one bound Ty reached Awai. He snatched her by her blouse with his tiger teeth, and caught her before she fell any farther down the hill.

As if she were just a child, he pulled her forward so that she was lying on the grass. For a moment Awai just stayed there, her heart pounding, blood rushing through her veins and throbbing in her head. She was so lucky that he'd caught her. That drop down the hillside could have been deadly.

The tiger lowered himself to the ground beside her and licked her cheek with his rough tongue. *I am sorry, tigress. Had I but thought—the cliff—sometimes I am impulsive. It is a fault I work daily to overcome.*

"You saved me." Awai eased up so that she was sitting beside Ty the tiger, her heart still pounding. "Okay, so a weretiger can come in handy now and again."

He was resting on his side, and on his belly was the pattern of a black club. She reached out and stroked it, and he purred. It was a low, rumbling purr that sent a thrill through her, making her body tingle and her clit throb.

“I’m not ready to give you an answer, Ty.” Awai slid her fingers down his belly, then away from him. She clenched her hands in her lap as she said, “The dominance thing . . . and this.” She gestured to him. “A weretiger? I’d be submitting to and fucking a weretiger?”

His rumbling chuckle filled her thoughts and reverberated through her like a miniorgasm.

But then he was transforming again. This time from tiger to man with the white and black hair vanishing or in some cases returning to clothing as he shifted to a sitting position. His long blond hair again flowed over his shoulders, his rogue’s smile teasing her as he sat close to her with one arm propped on his knee.

“I am as much a man as I am a weretiger,” he murmured as he caught a tendril of her dark hair between his thumb and forefinger. “And you will most definitely be fucking this man.”

CHAPTER FOUR

After Ty helped Awai brush the dirt, grass, and leaves from her clothing, he scooped up her whip and escorted her to the palace. Unlike the Awai who took the world by storm, she felt out of her element, unsure of what to do or how to act. When they entered the walls and passed the king's subjects within the sweeping hallways, she and Ty were met by respectful bows and curious glances.

Like Ty, the men mostly wore leather breeches, some with lace-up leather shirts and others bare-chested. The women were dressed in form-fitting robes, and it was obvious by their prominent nipples that they didn't wear bras. Heck, Awai didn't see any panty lines, so they probably didn't wear underwear, either.

The bedroom he led her to was expansive and airy, and absolutely perfect. A circular bed was the centerpiece of the room, and all the furnishings were rounded and curved. There was even a bookcase hugging one rounded wall. The wood was glossy and brown, like oak, only a much richer color. The room's covers and furnishings mimicked the shades of the hillside. Cherry blossom white, rich greens, and deep reds. It was as if the room itself were made of spring.

Ty tossed her whip onto the bed and Awai moved to one of the huge windows that led to a balcony. The windows reminded her of her condo in San Francisco, only here there were no skyscrapers in this view. The sun peeked through blue-green clouds, the rolling hills were covered in blossoms, and the bustling village sprawled across the valley below.

She felt Ty's presence before he spoke. "This is my kingdom, and it will be yours as well."

Despite the arrogance in his statement, Awai looked over her shoulder and cocked an eyebrow. "My queendom, you mean? After all, I am the Domme."

He gave a low chuckle that came out as a rumble. He kissed the curve of her neck, causing her to sigh. "I will teach you that submitting to me will fulfill your deepest needs and heal your heart and soul. Trust me, tigress. Let me tame you."

Ty turned her toward him while he pulled at the neck of her blouse and revealed her shoulder. She caught her breath as he licked a path from her neck all the way down the soft skin. "What if I don't want to be tamed?" she whispered.

He raised his head, a feral look in his blue gaze. "You will be mine, Awai. You will always be allowed to make your own choice . . . and you will choose to be my queen."

"You sure are a cocky SOB," she said with a tilt of her head. "If I make the choice to submit to you, it'll be just for sex and nothing more. So you might as well give up on the queen thing."

"We shall see, my tigress." He smiled, and in the next moment a woman came through the open doorway bearing a platter filled with food.

"Thank you, sorceress," Ty said to the woman who set the tray on a table in the corner of the room.

"My pleasure, Majesty," the woman murmured and gave a low bow. She was gorgeous with black hair and amber eyes, a voluptuous figure, and a form-fitting black robe.

"The sorceress Kalina will attend to your needs and your bath." Ty caught Awai's hand and brushed his lips across the back of it in a touch so light it caused her to shiver. "I will return on the morrow."

Awai danced among the cherry blossoms, spinning and spinning. Blooms swirled around her in a sweetly scented whirlwind. Her soul felt truly free . . . finally free.

A pure white tiger joined Awai, the large cat rolling in the blooms with the same sense of joy. It was as if the cat had escaped its cage and was reveling in its newfound freedom.

Darkness swept down on them, fast and sudden.

The malevolent presence caused Awai's heart to thunder and her blood to chill as if cold rain ran through her veins.

The white tiger spun on Awai, its eyes glowing a fierce red. The beast growled and slowly stalked toward Awai . . .

"No!" Awai was reaching for her whip at her bedside at the same moment she realized she'd been dreaming.

She flopped back on her pillow and stared at the ceiling, her heart pounding and the dream still vivid in her mind. The room she was in was dark, save for the glow of a single fat candle beside her bed. She turned toward it and frowned. Why did she leave a candle burning?

And then it all came back to her. Ty, the palace, his stories about her nieces and their children, his being a weretiger.

Ice slid over her and she tried to tell herself that had all been a dream, too. But even in the dim candlelight she could see that she was in unfamiliar surroundings. The same room that Ty and Kalina had left her in last night.

She started to climb out of bed and froze when she saw a gigantic tiger stretched out on the floor, its blue eyes focused on her.

Sleep, tigress, came Ty's voice, calm and soothing in her mind.

Awai scrambled under her covers and pulled them over her head. "It's all a dream. Only a dream," she whispered.

When Awai woke again, it was morning and she realized at once she was definitely not dreaming. She was in some kind of wonderland, with a gorgeous man who claimed she was to be his queen.

Yeah, right. That was sane.

After a servant brought in breakfast and Awai ate, she dressed and began pacing the room Ty had left her in.

Sunshine bathed the chamber as the sun rose over the hills. A cool breeze blew in through an open window, stiffening her nipples through the thin cotton of her blouse.

She'd disregarded the robes laid out for her and instead had put her own clothing back on. Last night she'd washed her underwear out and hung it up to dry. Her blouse and skirt were still clean, so she figured she'd wear them until she could find something more suitable to wear, like a shirt and pants. She wasn't about to dress in clinging robes that showed off her body like the other women wore in this place. Maybe the robes weren't so bad, but she felt a need to have some kind of control.

When she finally went to bed last night she'd wondered where Ty had gone. What if he'd slept with another woman? There were plenty of beauties in this place from what she'd seen when he escorted her through the palace. Not to mention the sorceress who had brought her dinner and had drawn her bath.

Awai frowned at the jealousy that pooled in her belly. She'd been in enough one-night stand BDSM relationships to care less about any man in particular. She'd never allowed herself to become attached to any one person, and had avoided personal intimacy. Sexual intimacy was one thing, but allowing a sub to know anything about her life outside the clubs was something she'd never permitted. The fact that she'd shared so much with Ty yesterday—that blew her away.

Then Awai remembered the dream about cherry blossoms and a pure white tiger and she paused in her pacing. Ty had been sleeping beside her bed in his tiger form and had spoken in her mind again. Something about his voice had been calming enough that she'd fallen asleep again.

"Are you ready to submit to me, tigress?" came Ty's deep penetrating voice from the doorway.

Awai whirled to face Ty and to see that he was even more incredibly handsome than she remembered. Again he was wearing only his leather pants and lace-up boots, and his long blond hair fell freely about his shoulders. She wanted to drop to her knees right then and there and say, "Take me, Master!"

And by the cocky look in his blue eyes, she had no doubt he could read the desire in her eyes.

"I need suitable clothes." She gestured toward the silky black robe lying over a clothing trunk. "That isn't what I call suitable."

Ty raised one eyebrow. "In the palace, it is what women wear. And when you agree to be my submissive, you will wear what I choose for you."

Before she could take the argument any further, he gave her that sexy little smile of his that made her heart melt a little more. He held out his hand and suddenly in his grasp was a pair of short boots. He handed them to her, and she found they were lined with something soft like sheepskin, and once she slipped them on, she discovered they actually looked good with her short skirt.

"Come," he said as he reached for her hand. "Let me show you more of my realm."

Surprisingly, Awai found herself looking forward to learning more about this world that she and her nieces were in. Although she had yet to discover their collective well-being, somehow she trusted Ty when he said they were doing well, that they were healthy, and cripes, that they were happy as mothers and wives.

I must be out of my mind. Since when did she trust the word of someone who was a virtual stranger to her?

Ty led her through the palace and then took her down a winding path. The air smelled of sunshine, wet earth, crisp pine, flowers, and other scents she couldn't identify.

He took Awai to his village first, and in her short skirt and midriff blouse, she felt extremely underdressed compared to the women of the village. Most wore robes, although many also wore shirts and leather pants. She was beginning to wish she'd worn the robe.

The village was an amazing place filled with color, music, laughter, and magic. She spent her time absorbing her surroundings while Ty spoke with his subjects and as he showed her the various shops. People bowed when he passed, and it was obvious in their motions and in their expressions that they respected and loved their king.

Was he showing her all this to impress her? Awai's old suspicions plagued her as she studied the man, but her instinct told her no.

He wasn't making an attempt to impress. He was simply sharing what had meaning, showing her his heart.

It was almost more than she could stand, considering she wanted to keep all inner walls firmly in place.

While he talked with the swordmaster about the order of weapons she was making for him, Awai took in the sights and sounds and scents of the village to distract herself. Warm smells of baked bread and cookies came from the bakery, and the smell of fresh fish from the fishmonger's. A cart filled with round and oblong fruits passed by. Behind it was a woman who seemed to be directing the cart with flicks of her wrist, but she wasn't actually touching the cart.

Magic. This whole place is powered by a force I don't even understand . . .

Awai's eyes strayed back to Ty, who indeed appeared to be a mysterious force as he admired the swordmaster's blades. The muscles in his arms bulged and rippled as he lifted a white-gold dagger. The sun's reflections on the blade were the same color as his hair. Indeed, she had never seen a man so beautiful, or so . . . basic. Ty seemed to have no artifice about him at all.

Enough! That can't be true. All men can deceive, and any man might. Shaking her head, Awai forced herself back to reality. Whatever that was.

For lunch they ate at an outdoor deli of sorts where their food appeared on the table before them. While they ate the spicy meat-filled pastries, Ty and Awai talked. He explained to her in more detail about his world and how their systems of trade worked and what his kingdom's specialties were. It was obvious he was proud of his people and his kingdom and Awai found herself admiring him even more, despite her best intentions not to let him get any closer.

After they'd finished eating, Ty took Awai up the hill and into the sweeping fall of cherry blossoms. At first it brought back the memory of her dream, but she brushed it away, not wanting to ruin the day just because she'd had a nightmare.

They walked through the grove, blossoms raining down and floating on the wind like small flurries of snow. Awai laughed as they caressed her face and landed in her hair. When she saw Ty's flower-studded hair she gave a little schoolgirl giggle, then clamped her hand over her mouth.

Ty smiled and brought her into his embrace. Without hesitation, he kissed her. A soft, slow kiss that soon deepened until her head was spinning and her body was crying out for him. She wanted him to take her here in the cherry blossoms, here where they were still in view of the palace, where she would do whatever he asked of her.

She broke the kiss. "You were serious . . ." Awai swallowed, then continued. "If I become your submissive, and I'm uncomfortable with anything, I can tell you and you won't push me?"

"I would never hurt you, my sweet tigress." His expression was sincere and caring. "As you no doubt know, any responsible Dominant dedicates himself—or herself—to caring for the needs of the submissive. Look into your heart, your instincts, and ask yourself if you feel that I would meet those needs."

She looked up at him, confused yet certain all at the same time. Maybe she was out of her mind, but he was giving her the choice. And she believed him when he said he would never push her beyond what she was comfortable with.

Was he right, too, that she needed to submit to fully heal her wounds?

And what about fulfilling my deepest fantasies, the ones I've never told anyone . . . barely even myself . . .

Awai bit her lower lip then slowly nodded. "All right. I'll give it a try."

The most sexy, seductive smile broke across Ty's face. He slid his hand into her hair and roughly brought her to him, this time kissing her hard and demanding, like she'd never been kissed before. Everything around her whirled. She'd never been so lost, so totally immersed in a kiss before. It gave her that shivery excited feeling that she'd always heard about but had never truly experienced until this very moment.

His intoxicating male scent surrounded her, mingling with the perfume of cherry blossoms and . . . pipe tobacco?

Ty pulled away from her, groaned, and put his forehead against hers. "Pillar."

Awai's mouth still felt hot and warm from his kiss, her senses still swirling. "Excuse me?"

"He means me, missy," a squeaky voice said.

Her gaze shot in the direction of the voice and to her surprise she saw a small man sitting cross-legged on a gigantic toadstool that was as high as her waist, the top at least twice the size of her hips. The man was smoking a long pipe that looked similar to a peace pipe. The scent of the tobacco was making her woozy . . . and very horny for Ty.

"Welcome to Clubs," Ty said with a bow to the little

man. He turned to Awai. "Câter Pillar is of the Munchfolk. Apparently he has chosen to grace us with his presence as well as the *cerih* pipe."

Awai almost giggled at the thought of the pipe-smoking caterpillar on the mushroom in *Alice in Wonderland*, but she managed to keep a straight face as she said, "Nice to meet you, Mr. Pillar."

"Just Pillar." The man extended his short arm toward Awai, holding out the pipe. "One puff each and I'll be off!"

"Er . . ." Awai looked up at Ty and he gave her a firm nod. As she turned back to the little man and took the pipe, it occurred to her that she was already deferring to Ty as her Dom. That caused her a moment's hesitation, but then she realized she had already told him she would be his submissive.

"Thank you, Pillar," she said, not at all sure she was thankful as she brought the pipe to her lips. But when she took a puff of the cherry-flavored tobacco, her entire body responded. Just being with Ty had already made her hot and wet for him, but something about this *cerih* pipe made her beyond aroused. She wanted to jump Ty now, caterpillar man be damned.

Her eyes were heavy-lidded as she handed the pipe to Ty. He smiled, his gaze appraising nipples that raised the material of her thin shirt. He puffed on the pipe then returned the long device to Pillar.

The little man stood on the mushroom, gave a flourishing bow, then the next thing Awai knew, she was staring at a few sparkles.

Pillar was gone.

"How'd he do that?" She looked up at Ty, who had his arms folded across his chest.

"He is Munchfolk. It is the way of their people." His expression went completely serious. "You are certain you wish to submit to me?"

Awai nodded. She'd clearly made up her mind before the woozy horny feeling she was experiencing right now. "Yes."

His features hardened into those of a true Dom. "You will refer to me as Your Majesty, or simply Majesty." His sapphire blue eyes darkened as he added, "starting from this very moment."

Well, damn. He certainly wasn't taking any time getting into his role. Awai bit back a retort, automatically wanting to reject his demands. Of course she had insisted her subs refer to her as Mistress, so this situation was certainly no different.

"Yes, Your Majesty," she murmured and lowered her eyes. To her surprise the submissiveness of the act aroused her.

Within her line of sight, he gestured to the moss-covered tree behind her. "Move so that your back is against it and raise your hands above your head."

She shivered with excitement at the command in his tone, but did as he ordered. The *cerih* pipe had made her relaxed and languid, and she felt any of her remaining inhibitions draining away.

When she was against the tree, her hands high, Ty held

out his hand and two lengths of golden rope appeared in his palm.

"How do you do that?" she blurted. Ty frowned, and she added, "Your Majesty."

"It is a talent of my people." He reached for her hands, which she still held above her head. "In the future do not ask questions unless you have asked for permission first."

A moment of fear passed through Awai as he bound her hands to the tree. Her voice trembled a little as she said, "Yes, Majesty."

Ty fastened the second length of rope around her waist so that she was tied firmly to the tree. When he was finished, he studied her as though she were a fine portrait, then reached up and pushed her blouse so that it was above her nipples. Cool air brushed the taut nubs and Awai bit her lip to keep from moaning.

Ty gave a satisfied nod then held out his hand again. On his palm appeared a pair of gold club charms. He leaned down and flicked his tongue over one of her nipples, causing her to gasp. In the next moment he was fastening one of the charms over her nipple and pulling the loop taut. The hard nub quickly turned purple, engorged with blood. Awai squirmed from the pain and pleasure of it. He slipped another nipple ring on her other breast and this time she arched up to him, pulling against her bonds, begging him for more.

Awai could swear Ty was purring like a tiger as he cupped both her breasts and flicked his tongue against one nipple while tweaking the other with his fingers. She yanked against her bonds, wanting to touch him, to unfasten his pants and to slip his cock out so that she could ride him. She never knew how exciting it was to be tied up and under someone else's control—someone she didn't fear and hate.

His mouth and hand left her nipples and she whimpered as his tongue slowly traveled from between her breasts to her belly button. He knelt as he licked her falling-star charm then slid his tongue inside her navel.

"Majesty!" Awai gasped as the sensation traveled straight to her pussy and caused her juices to flow along the inside of one thigh.

"Quiet, tigress," he murmured while he slid each of her half boots off and tossed them aside. He pushed her skirt up around her waist then slid her thong down to her ankles.

It was so erotic to be on a hillside with his palace in view . . . practically naked . . . to feel her panties around her feet, to have her pussy exposed to Ty's gaze, to have the charms keeping her nipples hard. And that puff from the *cerih* pipe made the experience even more exciting.

When he scented her, she trembled, waiting for his mouth to go down on her slit, to taste her. With his fingers he spread her lips and Awai felt cool air over her clit. Then with a single swipe of his tongue, she almost came.

"So sweet your juices flow for me." He nuzzled her bare mound. "You wish for my cock. You desire me."

Awai pulled against her bonds, feeling wanton and excited and more turned on than she'd ever been in her life.

"Tell me," he demanded. "What do you want?"

"I want you to fuck me, Majesty." Awai loved saying the word "fuck." She reveled in it, the hard sexual sound of the word and what it meant.

He growled with obvious pleasure. "Later I will give you my cock." He licked her mound that she kept waxed and smooth. "For now it pleases me to taste you."

When he laved her clit again, she moaned. Her voice trembled as she said, "I'm going to come, Majesty."

"You may not climax without my permission." His blue eyes met hers as he paused, leaving her hanging at the edge. "Or I shall have to punish you."

Well, that certainly came as no surprise. She'd done that to her submissives a hundred times.

A sensual thrill shot through her belly as she wondered what kind of punishment he had in mind for her. The way she was feeling, so relaxed and uninhibited, she was ready for anything and everything.

Ty grabbed her silky thong. His muscles flexed as he easily ripped the material and tossed it into a patch of flowers. He placed his hands on her ass and lifted her so that her feet no longer reached the ground. "Hook your legs over my shoulders," he commanded.

Awai obeyed him as he helped her. Now she was hanging from the golden ropes with nothing to keep her from dropping but the rope and Ty.

When she was spread out before him, her pussy open and at the same level as his mouth, Ty began devouring her. Oh, god, it felt good having him eat out her pussy. He thrust two fingers into her channel as he sucked and licked her. And then to her amazement, he slid a finger from his other hand into her ass. She'd used dildos and butt plugs in her ass before, but having Ty thrust into her this way was even more arousing.

She gasped as waves of heat rushed over her body, from her toes to the roots of her hair, telling her that she was close to orgasm. "I'm going to climax, Your Majesty. Please let me come."

"No." He muttered the word as he continued to fuck her pussy and her ass with his fingers and lick her clit. It was like he had an extra pair of hands the way he was able to do what he was doing.

And then he did the most amazing thing—he growled against her pussy, sending vibration after vibration of pleasure through her body. Her thighs began to tremble, and she clenched his head tight between her knees.

Awai arched her back, struggling to control her hips, fighting off the orgasm that was building and building, driving her mad with the need to come.

As she squirmed on his shoulders, she looked up to see two bare-chested gorgeous men—one with golden hair, the other with black—mere feet away. They had huge bulges in their pants, their arms were folded across their chests.

They were watching her and Ty.

CHAPTER FIVE

THE SIGHT OF THE TWO MEN WATCHING TY LICKing her pussy threw Awai over the edge into an orgasm of gigantic proportion. A shout ripped from her throat as her climax rocked her body. Like a firestorm, heat flushed over her from head to toe and burned beneath her skin. Her hips pumped against Ty's face as she stared wide-eyed at the two men who studied them with obvious satisfaction and arousal.

"Ty." She could hardly take a breath and she couldn't take her eyes from the golden-haired man with the kingly bearing or the rough, dark man to his side. "There—there are two men watching us."

Ty slid her legs from his shoulders and settled her bare feet on the ground. If she wasn't still tied to the tree, she was sure she would have fallen because her legs didn't want to hold her up.

Without looking at the men, Ty's eyes met hers. "You have now earned two punishments, Awai."

"Two?" she blurted, but clamped her mouth shut at Ty's stony expression.

"You climaxed without permission and you referred to me by my name," he said sternly.

But what about the men? She wanted to scream the words, but she was afraid he'd add another punishment.

"Yes, Majesty," she murmured, trying not to look at the men who stood silently by.

As Ty slowly got to his feet Awai's nipples ached and her pussy dripped moisture just from knowing the men had watched them. And the fact that they were still looking at her body with hungry expressions caused her to be even more excited.

The puff from the *cerih* pipe also made it easier to admit to the fantasy she'd been having so often lately.

What would it be like to have sex with all three of them? To fulfill those fantasies?

Because of the hazy, relaxed feeling the pipe had given her, it was like she had no inhibitions at all any longer. It was what she wanted, and she could admit that now to herself. Maybe even to Ty.

Awai rolled her eyes to the lacey green leaves above her. She didn't even know who these men were and yet she was fantasizing about having them and Ty all at once.

Her man—her king now that she had pledged to be his submissive—took her chin in his hand and forced her to look at him again. He brushed his lips across hers and she caught her scent on his mouth and tasted her flavor on his lips. "Remember, my tigress, you must follow my rules. You must do whatever it is I tell you to do, unless it is beyond your comfort level. Do you understand?"

Awai nodded. "Yes, Majesty."

Ty released his hold on her chin and turned to the men. "Lord Kir." He gave a deep nod to the golden-haired man. "Rafe," he said to the dark, untamed looking rogue, giving him a nod as well. Awai stared in amazement as Ty greeted them like it was no big deal, as if it was perfectly normal for the men to watch Ty giving oral sex . . .

Maybe it's something they've done before. Maybe Ty planned it. The thought made the skin prickle at her nape, but then her anger vanished as she realized how much she had enjoyed it. How much she liked having them look at her now, her skirt up around her waist and her blouse above her breasts, completely exposed to their gazes.

No wonder subs got off on this. The experience was powerful. She had total control over the arousals of these three men.

"I did not expect you for several days yet," Ty was saying to the men, bringing her attention back to the conversation.

"We were hunting in your woods," the man named Lord Kir said, giving Awai an untamed smile as his gaze traveled over her exposed body. "But we heard sounds we were compelled to investigate."

I'll bet you did, Awai thought, shivering beneath Kir's intent perusal.

He stepped so close that she caught his scent of forest

and something far more wild. "May I touch this fair one?" Kir murmured.

Awai's gaze shot to Ty to see him give a slow nod, his golden earring catching the late morning sunlight. "This one is special, Kir. Awai is to be my Queen."

Her eyes widened. "Wha—" she started, but at his frown she shut her mouth and turned her attention back to the golden-haired man who was reaching for her.

"Ah, yes," Kir said as his warm hands cupped both her breasts. "She is a beautiful find, indeed." Gently he caressed the full globes, his calloused fingers sending thrills straight from her chest to her pussy. She had to bite her lower lip to keep from moaning. But when he tugged on her nipple rings, Awai couldn't hold back a whimper of pleasure.

Kir gave a satisfied smile and stepped back. When she glanced at Ty, his face was a mask and she could only wonder how he felt about other men touching her. Part of her wanted him to be jealous, but part of her wanted to know what it was like to enjoy the pleasures of three men at once—and to know that Ty would enjoy seeing her pleasured.

The dark and brooding man called Rafe moved to where Kir had been standing a moment before. He raised an eyebrow at Ty.

Ty gave a slow nod but this time there was a predatory look to his blue eyes. As if he didn't trust Rafe.

Rafe's mouth quirked and it made him look more dangerous than ever. Awai trembled as the man reached up and slipped his hand into her hair then brushed his lips slowly over hers. She tasted his breath and felt its warmth upon her lips. He gently nipped at her lower lip, causing Awai to gasp just before he pulled away.

Ty narrowed his eyes and wondered if he could truly share Awai with his brothers-at-arms. If Awai wished to enjoy the pleasures of three men at once, he would allow it.

But only once.

And definitely not at this moment. Not before he had her completely to himself.

When Rafe stepped back, Ty caught a loose strand of Awai's hair in his fist. He knew the *cerih* would allow her to speak freely of her soul's desires. It would only compel her to tell him what she wished him to know, but no further. If she desired something but did not want him to know, then it would remain her secret.

Ty tugged on Awai's hair, causing her to gasp. "Would you enjoy having three cocks at once, my tigress?"

"If it pleases you . . ." Awai's eyes locked with his, and he could see the intense desire burning in her gaze. "It is one of my fantasies, Your Majesty."

Kir and Rafe both gave low rumbles, and Ty smiled despite the jealousy that threatened to drive him to pummel his brothers-at-arms. He had never been jealous before, and had always enjoyed sharing women with Kir and Rafe or his brothers. It was an enticing sight, to see a woman being pleasured in every way.

"Then that wish shall be fulfilled." He turned to Kir and Rafe and spoke in the old werewolf language, instructing them. "*Rorah dumai catuch.*"

Both men gave low bows. "It will be," Lord Kir said.

Awai stared with surprise as the men transformed into gorgeous wolves . . . skin to fur, arms to legs, and bushy tails. Kir was blue-eyed and a gorgeous golden color, and Rafe was black as the darkest of nights with equally black eyes. With amazing grace and speed, the two bounded into the woods and vanished.

She turned back to Ty and saw his expression of desire, yet was that jealousy?

"Well, you asked," she murmured. "Your Majesty."

"Indeed I did." He smiled and hooked his finger under her chin. "It gives me great pleasure to know your fantasy will be fulfilled . . . one time and one time only."

After they returned to the palace, Ty took Awai on a tour. She enjoyed exploring the bright rooms, from his extensive library and his den, to the bathing rooms and bedchambers, to the servants' quarters and kitchen.

The palace was filled with living and growing things . . . plants with green leaves, some with red leaves, and still others with blue. Flowers tumbled from small alcoves above and around them, the blooms in shades of white, red, purple, pink, and orange.

Ty's palace seemed an extension of the hills around them, bright and filled with undeniable happiness. Even his servants walked by with smiles and laughter, but always with respect and reverence for their king, and Ty seemed all the more impressive and powerful.

Awai was amazed at how comfortable she felt with Ty.

While they strolled through the palace, he invited her to tell him about her life in San Francisco and about her nieces. They laughed over the stories Awai told and Ty shared with her his experiences with her nieces.

Part of Awai felt left out, not having been with them as they experienced this world, their marriages, and their children. But another part of her was proud of her nieces and so pleased that they were happy. Her gut told her that Ty was telling her the truth, and her gut instincts were what got her to the top rung of the advertising ladder.

When it was late, Ty again left her alone in her room. "Be prepared," he murmured before he left. "Tomorrow I will begin your training."

The following morning, Ty entered Awai's bedchamber with Kalina, the beautiful dark-haired woman, at his side. "Kalina will prepare you for me today, tigress."

He took the sorceress's hand and brushed his lips over her knuckles. "She has served Tarok for many years and is most loyal to all our kingdoms."

Awai's gut clenched as the gorgeous woman gave a small bow and a secret smile to Ty. "As always it has been my pleasure."

Jealousy almost caused Awai to break her oath of obedience and kick the woman's ass—and Ty's. Instead she managed to keep her face a calm mask, even though her hands were fisted at her sides.

Ty released the sorceress's fingers and had to hold back a grin at his future mate's obvious discomfort. It was a good sign that she did not wish for another woman to touch him. He could sense it in every manner of Awai's bearing, even in her scent.

"Do as the sorceress instructs," he said with a firm look at Awai. "She will ensure you are ready for me."

Awai bit the inside of her lip to keep from telling him to fuck off. "Yes, Your Majesty," she murmured as docilely as possible.

He gave a kingly nod, turned on his heel, and strode out the door.

"First a bath," Kalina said as she started for the bathing room attached to the chamber. "The king instructed that you use special soaps to relax your body for him," she added as Awai followed.

The sorceress's words sent a shiver down Awai's spine. Her body was being conditioned for Ty as if she was his property.

Which, in fact, she was. As long as she chose to submit to him, she belonged to Ty.

The bathing room was gorgeous—made of marble, crystal, and glass, with a ninety-degree view of the flower-strewn hillside and wash of cherry blossoms. The crystal tub at the center of the room rose up from the green marbled floor, and Awai could see the steamy water through the clear sides.

After she stripped off her clothing and handed them to the sorceress, Awai started for the tub. She was not embarrassed at being seen naked. She had a taut, firm body and enjoyed appreciative glances. Kalina was no exception, her amber eyes watching every move Awai made.

She eased up the crystal steps, climbed into the tub, and slid into the incredibly warm cherry blossom perfumed water. "Oh, god, this is heaven." Awai sighed as she relaxed against the smooth side of the tub and stared out at the amazing view.

Awai allowed herself to be pampered while the sorceress washed her hair with almond-scented shampoo, and then bathed her with a soft sponge and a gel that smelled like whipped cream and cocoa.

Good lord, I'm an ice cream sundae. Awai smirked. Maybe Ty would want to sample a little of everything she had.

When Awai had finished bathing, the sorceress dried her off in a thick, soft, white towel with Ty's club crest embroidered on it, then set the towel aside.

"Sit here." Kalina pointed to a crystal bench close to one of the windows.

Awai slipped onto the bench and felt its coolness beneath her bare ass and pussy. Kalina wore her clinging black robe, but Awai was still naked. She wasn't ashamed or embarrassed. Quite the opposite. She found she enjoyed the excitement of being naked when others were clothed—much like how her subs had enjoyed being naked when she was fully dressed. With the club charms still dangling from her nipples, the nubs were tight and hard. Her skin glistened, damp from the steamy room.

Kalina retrieved a crystal brush from a small table nearby, moved behind Awai, and began brushing her hair with slow methodical strokes. In no time at all, her hair was dry . . . like magic. Awai shivered, her excitement mounting from being "prepared" to go to Ty.

"You are a beautiful woman," Kalina said as she came around to stand before Awai. The sorceress's nipples were erect through her silky black robe and Awai wondered if Kalina wore nipple rings, too. "The king is right—your eyes are as blue as the leaves of a *ch'tok.*"

Awai gestured to one of the feathery blue-leaved trees outside the window. "Is that a *ch'tok*?"

"Yes, Milady." Kalina reached for a clear pot filled with a red creamy mixture. "The tree has magical properties."

Before Awai had a chance to ask the sorceress about the magic of the tree and other magic she'd seen, Kalina was dabbing the crimson substance from the jar on Awai's lips. It felt like lipstick and smelled of cherries.

Kalina smoothed a bit of the red stuff on each of Awai's cheeks, and Awai was afraid she was going to look like a total slut wearing too much makeup. "Do you have a mirror around here?" she asked as Kalina stepped back to look at her handiwork.

"When I'm finished." Kalina dipped a finger into the pot and surprised Awai by dabbing the mixture onto one of her nipples, around the charm, and covering the areola.

"I'm going to look like a tart," Awai said as her gaze shot from her nipple to the sorceress.

Kalina grinned. "Strawberry or cherry?"

Awai had to laugh. "Today, definitely cherry."

The sorceress made Awai close her eyes, then applied shadow to her lids and lash line. As she applied the makeup, Kalina explained how Awai was to greet King Ty and how she should stand as she waited for him to acknowledge her.

When she was finished with the makeup, Kalina placed a mirror in Awai's hands. "You may open your eyes now, Milady."

Mirror, mirror on the wall . . .

Awai held her breath, afraid she was going to see a cheap tramp looking back at her. What she saw in the crystal-framed oval mirror would have put any Nordstrom's makeup artist to shame. Her makeup was perfectly applied, subtle, yet artful. Her eyes appeared larger and bluer, her mouth full and lush, her cheekbones prominent, and her nipples . . . Well, they looked hot and she knew that Ty was going to love them.

Next came the clothing, and Awai's excitement level mounted. The top was a three-inch white leather strap that wrapped around her breasts and was fastened in the back and barely hid her rouged nipples and nipple charms. The white leather skirt was so tiny that it came well below her star charm at her belly button, and went only to the top of her thighs, barely covering her waxed mound. Next Kalina handed Awai a pair of thigh-high boots that would have done any Dominatrix proud. They were made of the supplest, softest white leather, and reached about mid-thigh.

When she stood in front of a full-length mirror in the bedroom, Awai figured she looked so hot that she'd do herself if she were a man. Or hell, a woman even. Her dark hair flowed around her shoulders, her complexion creamy and beautiful, her makeup perfect.

I look like another woman . . . in another world.

Behind Awai the sorceress smiled at their reflections and said, “Yes, the king has chosen well.”

CHAPTER SIX

TY PACED THE FLOOR LIKE A CAGED TIGER AS HE waited in the breakfast chamber for his woman. He had no doubt she would choose to be his mate. Awai had already chosen, whether she realized it or not.

His boots thunked against the marble floor as he walked the length of the majestic dining table and back again. Beneath the white linen cloth was a table made of the finest crystal, with ten carved chairs from the same precious substance with white cushions. A swirling red vase graced the center of the table, and cherry blossoms spilled over its edges and onto the white tablecloth.

He paused in his pacing, stood with his feet square with his shoulders, hands behind his back, and stared out the window and down at his village. When he had taken Awai to the village yesterday, he was certain his subjects had been as taken with her as he was.

From behind him came Awai's smooth as velvet voice. "Your Majesty."

Ty hesitated only a moment, that fraction of time that a ruler used to show he was in control. But when he turned and saw Awai, he almost lost all that control.

As in he nearly climaxed in his breeches.

Her lips were curled into a seductive smile, her chin high, her stance wide, and her hands were behind her back as Kalina had surely instructed her. But her eyes sparkled with something that told him she knew what she was doing to him at that very moment.

Ty ordered his cock to stand down, and gritted his teeth when it refused to cooperate. His leather breeches were far too tight and little blood was making its way to his brain. So instead he focused on controlling his woman.

"Sit to my right," he ordered her, gesturing to the seat beside his own at the head of the massive dining table.

"Yes, Majesty," she said with her eyes lowered, a hint of a smile still curving her luscious lips.

Cool air brushed his naked chest as he pulled the high-backed chair out for her, then seated himself. In moments servants and chefs appeared, placing before Ty and Awai platters of roasted fowl, baked bread, vegetables, fruits, and pastries.

Once their plates were filled by one of the servants, Ty inclined his head to Awai. "You may eat now, my tigress."

"Thank you, Majesty." Awai speared a piece of a meat and vegetable-filled pastry with her fork.

Ty took that moment to place his hand on her knee and slowly slide it upward to the inside of her thigh. Awai froze in mid-motion, her eyes wide as he moved up farther, closer to her mound.

"Go ahead, my sweet," Ty murmured close to her ear. "Eat."

Awai tensed as Ty's hand settled on her thigh.

"Eat," he commanded again, and she started in slowly on the unusual food items on her plate. His hand remained close to her bare mound, and she had a hard time focusing on the meal or the conversation. He did mention sending messengers out to inform the kings and queens, telling them that Awai was now with him, but Ty did not know when his brothers and her nieces would arrive. Likely not for a few weeks.

With Ty's hand teasing her mound, Awai's desire for him increased by the second. By the time they finished their meal, she was so ready for him that she wanted to jump the man.

When she set down her fork and looked up at him, Ty said, "The dungeon awaits. Follow me," as he pushed back his chair and strode out of the dining chamber.

Awai's belly flip-flopped as she wondered what he had in store for her. *I've been in countless dungeons*, she reminded herself as she slipped out of her chair to follow him. *This one can't be any different.*

Ty walked ahead of her, the muscles of his naked back flexing with every powerful movement he made. His long blond hair flowed well past his shoulders, and the black leather pants molded his tight ass.

She couldn't wait to get him out of them.

Maybe it was because she was used to the Dom/sub

relationships she had witnessed in the BDSM clubs, and the fact she'd been a Domme herself—whatever the case, it didn't bother Awai to walk behind Ty in a subservient manner. She had chosen this role—at least for now—and she intended to enjoy every aspect of it. She trusted that Ty would keep his word, and believed that if she was uncomfortable with anything, he would back off.

Although with everything she'd done to her subs—that they always enjoyed—and with everything she'd seen in other D/s relationships, she didn't think there was much she'd be uncomfortable with. The only place she wouldn't go was public humiliation or corporal punishment. Safe, sane, and consensual, always.

Awai followed Ty through the airy palace. Warm sunshine poured in through countless windows and her boots made soft thunks on the marble tiles as she walked. Cool air caressed her naked shoulders, her belly, the undersides of her breasts, and the part of her thighs not covered by her skirt or her boots.

At the end of one long hallway, Ty reached a large green wooden door, stopped, and waited for Awai to catch up with him. She expected a dark winding staircase leading down to an even darker dungeon, but when Ty opened the door, the landing was brightly lit by skylights. The door closed softly behind them as she followed him down a wide set of green marble steps and into an expansive hallway. The floor was the same forest green marble, but the walls were white with many paintings of landscapes and seascapes. The sight of the paintings reminded Awai of Annie, and she couldn't help but wonder how her niece fared these days.

The hallway was also lit by skylights. They were positioned to one side of the hallway where Awai could see grass and flowers blooming outside. She realized they had to be underground, but not entirely beneath the castle.

They reached a set of double doors at the end of the hallway. Ty grasped the gold club-shaped handles and flung open the doors.

It was the most amazing "dungeon" Awai had ever seen. The lighting was more intimate, but not too dark, and everything was white instead of black. There were so many devices that Awai couldn't begin to absorb them all. She heard the door close behind her as her experienced eye ran over items that seemed traditional, like a St. Andrew's cross, spreader bars, seats with restraints, spanking benches, suspension gear, swings, a cage with glass bars, and much more.

Each item appeared to be different from what she was used to. Like the swing that hung from nothing, as if invisible restraints held it in midair. The St. Andrew's cross was the centerpiece of the room, but what was incredible was that it was made of crystal and it actually seemed to glow. She could sense a sort of power radiating from it. All the other items seemed somehow different, too, but she was too overwhelmed to take it all in.

Along two walls were assorted floggers, whips, canes, paddles, white leather restraints and harnesses, tethers, ticklers, blindfolds, candles, and that glittering golden rope he had used to tie her with earlier. It was all close to what she was familiar with, yet not.

"Wow," Awai said as she turned to look at Ty. At his frown, she lowered her eyes demurely and added, "Your Majesty."

Within her line of vision, he held out his hand. On his palm a black collar appeared, with a gold club charm dangling from it. The club matched the charms hanging from her nipples.

"Will you wear my collar to signify that you are mine?" he asked in a firm tone. "You will be my slave until I have broken through the barriers that hold your heart and soul hostage."

Awai paused, understanding the symbolism of the gesture, yet wondering if being his "slave" would help her heal. If she refused, this would end. But if she accepted the collar, then she also accepted whatever came next.

"Yes, Your Majesty," she finally said. "I accept your gift."

Ty moved behind her and she lifted her long dark hair so that he could fasten the collar around her neck. She shivered from the light brush of his fingertips against her neck as the charm swung against the hollow at the base of her throat.

When he was finished and she had turned back to him, she felt different somehow. A little nervous knowing she was truly this man's sub, and she must do all that he asked of her. But she also realized that she held power over him; she was responsible for his pleasure as he was responsible for caring for her.

Ty kept his expression serious as he held out his hand.

A whip appeared in his grip—another display of his magic—and then Awai realized it was hers. She'd left it in her bedchamber.

He snapped the whip and Awai jumped as the crack filled the room. "It is time for your first punishment, tigress."

She worried the inside of her lower lip as she glanced from the whip to Ty's face. He showed no emotion in his expression, but his eyes held warmth. She was certain he wouldn't hurt her.

Wasn't she?

"Yes, Majesty." She folded her hands behind her as Kalina had earlier instructed. "What would you have me do?"

"Remove your clothing." Ty held his hands behind his back, his head high, the club tattoo rippling at his abs. "But leave on your boots."

Awai felt a shiver of excitement trail up her spine. She had no compunctions about being naked in front of anyone, and especially this man. When she pulled the white leather strap covering her breasts over her head, a pained expression crossed Ty's features, but then it was gone. He seemed mesmerized by her breasts, unable to take his eyes from her rouged nipples.

But when she shimmied out of the leather skirt and kicked it aside, she saw his throat work, as though he was swallowing down his desires. The bulge in his leather pants was absolutely huge, and her nipples tightened just looking at it.

Ty cleared his throat and motioned with the whip to

the St. Andrews cross. "Stand facing the cross, with your back to me, *slave*."

The way he said *slave* turned her on beyond belief. "Yes, Your Majesty," Awai said, then moved to the crystal X at the center of the room. She purposely added a little extra sway to her hips, just for Ty's benefit. She loved the way it felt to be naked except for the thigh-high boots, her collar, and her nipple rings. The charms swayed against her breasts and at her neck, and the boots felt snug and supple around her legs.

When she reached the cross she stood, waiting for his instruction.

"Raise your arms," he commanded near her ear, surprising her because he was so close to her. How did he do that?

"Yes, Majesty." Awai complied, raising her arms so that they were splayed out at the top of the X. Ty produced a magical golden rope out of nowhere, slipped it through a clear hook on the X, and tied one wrist. He took his time, brushing his chest against her back and his arms against hers, in slow, sensuous movements that made her pussy flood with moisture. When he was finished, he repeated the process with her other wrist so that both arms were firmly secured, but in the same slow manner designed to drive her crazy with lust.

Awai took a deep breath as she waited for his next instruction. "Spread your legs," he said, and she obeyed. The restraints at her wrists allowed her to follow his instructions without losing her balance. He teased her by running his hands along the inside of one thigh, down her boot to her ankle before tying it to the cross with the golden rope. He tantalized her with every touch, his warm breath a caress upon her skin, and she swore she could feel the heat from his palms through the supple leather boots as he grasped her ankles.

The crystal cross felt surprisingly warm and comfortable against her cheek, her breasts, her belly, and her mound. Perhaps it was the white glow, but it was somehow relaxing—even though Ty was driving her out of her mind with need for him.

A whip cracked behind Awai and her heart beat faster as she realized she was about to be whipped. She swallowed down the rush of fear that tightened her chest, but she couldn't stop the sudden trembling in her body.

"What is wrong, my sweet tigress?" he murmured near her ear, his breath fanning her cheek as he spoke.

"I—I . . ." Awai couldn't believe she had such a hard time getting it out. She was a millionaire business woman for chrissake, and a former Domme. "Your Majesty, may I have a safe word?"

"What is a safe word?" From the sound of his voice he was clearly puzzled.

"It's a word we agree upon." Awai swallowed again. "If what's happening frightens me, hurts me, or is outside my comfort zone, I say the word and you stop immediately."

"Of course." He kissed her neck in that sensitive dip before her shoulder. "What would you like to be your safe word?"

Awai closed her eyes for a moment, then opened them. "Cherry blossoms."

"Then cherry blossoms it is." Ty gave a soft laugh that tickled her spine. "You have nothing to fear from me, my lovely. I am your king. I will take care of you and make sure you are safe, always."

"Thank you, Majesty," Awai whispered, and relaxed against the cross.

The rough feel of the leather whip trailed across her shoulders and back. "Do you know why you are being punished, slave?"

"Yes, Majesty." Awai shifted against her bonds. "I climaxed without your permission and I did not refer to you as you instructed me."

"That is correct, my beauty."

The whip slithered over her shoulder, across her breasts, and then up her neck. Awai sighed at the sensual feel of the whip gliding over her body. A nervous tingling, a sense of both anticipation and a little bit of fear, heated her body.

"You are as precious as the rarest of flowers," he murmured as he nuzzled her hair and continued to trail the whip over her body. "Like the cherry blossoms, you are to be treasured and loved in my kingdom."

Awai tensed at the word "love" but relaxed again as Ty moved away and skimmed her back and ass with the whip. She even felt it through the buttery soft leather of the thigh-high boots. Her body was relaxed against the cross, her golden bonds keeping her firmly tied to its surface.

When she realized the whip was no longer caressing her, she stiffened, waiting for the first blow. *Cherry blossoms,* she reminded herself. *If I don't enjoy this, all I have to say is "cherry blossoms."*

The lash landed across her butt cheeks, barely a kiss and a light sting. Again the lash fell, and again. Each lash was a little stronger than the last, but Awai found herself relaxing, then tensing in anticipation of each one. The pain and pleasure intermingled like chill wind on her cheeks on an icy cold day. Sharp at first, but then cool, and the bitter pain was welcome.

Desire grew within her as Ty whipped her, her pussy creamy with her juices, her nipples hard and aching from the nipple rings. It was an amazing feeling—this stinging pleasure that brought her closer to orgasm with every stroke.

When she was about to beg him to let her come, the lashes stopped. Awai sagged against her bonds, her body burning from the lashes and burning for Ty.

He moved behind her again, pushed her hair from her neck, and kissed her nape, just above her collar. "You look so beautiful standing here," he whispered. "Your body pink from my lashes, your juices glittering on your quim and on the inside of your thighs. Would you like me to fuck you now, slave?"

"Please." Awai wished she could turn into his arms, but her bonds held her tight. "Please, Your Majesty, fuck me."

He rubbed his palm over her ass and slipped his fingers into her creamy wetness. "Yes, you are ready for me."

Ty brought his fingers to his mouth and tasted Awai on his tongue. He wanted nothing more than to take her now, but he had to maintain his role, to show her how much she enjoyed being dominated by her king.

"I am not yet finished with your punishments, my sweet." He knelt and with his magic he removed the golden rope from around her booted ankle and from the cross. Once he made sure Awai's foot was firmly beneath her on the marbled floor, he repeated the process with her other ankle. Her legs trembled and he knew he would need to make sure she didn't fall when he released her.

As he rose, he kissed the bared flesh above her boots and lightly ran his tongue over her naked pussy lips. Awai moaned and arched toward him, but he only smiled and continued to work his way up over her firm ass to the sensitive spot at the base of her spine. She whimpered and then shivered as he ran his tongue from the crack of her ass, slowly up her spine to her shoulder blades. He gripped her waist with both hands and licked his way up to her neck again to the collar around her elegant throat.

"Are you ready to be freed from the cross?" he asked as he nestled his body tight to hers, his hard cock pressed to her lower back.

"Yes, Majesty," she murmured.

With a flick of his wrist, Ty removed the bonds and sent the golden ropes back to the table of his favorite pleasure toys. He caught Awai to him at the same moment he released her, holding her tight until he felt she was able to stand on her own.

He turned her to face him so that she was in his embrace. "Are you ready for your next punishment, my tigress?"

CHAPTER SEVEN

TY HELD BACK A SMILE FROM HIS FUTURE QUEEN. Awai's cheeks were flushed, her blue eyes wide as she looked up at him. "Yes, Majesty."

"That's a good girl." He took her arm and escorted her to the leather altar in one corner of the chamber. "Have you ever been punished with hot wax?"

Awai's gaze shot up to meet Ty's and a mixture of fear and excitement filled her again. "You mean wax play, Your Majesty?"

One of Ty's eyebrows rose a notch. "Perhaps." He patted the leather platform in front of her. "Climb onto the altar and lie on your back."

Awai did feel like a sacrificial virgin—er, woman—as she climbed onto the white padded leather altar. It was soft, the finest of leathers, and she figured that no sacrifice had ever felt so good.

Ty strapped her down, spread eagle, with those golden ropes he always made appear out of nowhere. As he had before, he used slow, sensual movements, tracing her legs and thighs with the ropes and with his fingertips. He even teased her nipples with the ropes and tugged at her nipple charms, adjusting the loops so that they were even firmer around her already taut nubs.

When she was splayed out for his enjoyment and her punishment, the nervousness in her belly increased. Ty produced a candle in his palm, another display of magic that seemed to come so naturally to him.

Ty flicked his fingers and a small flame burst atop the candle that was a deep shade of mulberry and smelled of raspberries when it started to burn. The flame flickered and danced, its bluish-yellow flame almost mesmerizing her.

Awai had never before felt as vulnerable as she did at that moment. Even being whipped on the cross had been different from being splayed out on this "altar." At least on the cross her back had been to him. Now he could see all of her—from her facial expressions to her rouged nipples, to her wide, open pussy.

"This is made from a special wax that is not too hot and will not harm your skin." He held the candle over one of her breasts. "Are you ready, tigress?"

She could already see the wax pooling at its top and a bead dripping down its side. "Yes, Majesty." He tilted the candle over her nipple and she shut her eyes tight, then gasped as the wax burned, then cooled . . . pain, then pleasure.

"Watch," he demanded, and she opened her eyes.

She looked up to see his blue gaze, as blue as the crystal waters in the Bahamas, and she became lost in those eyes. He could do anything to her and she knew she would enjoy it. All in that one moment she knew for a fact that he would never hurt her, would never cause her pain beyond what was enjoyable.

Her gaze followed his as he looked to her nipple and dribbled wax over the taut nub and the nipple ring. Again the burning feeling and then a sense of bliss as the wax rolled down her firm globe to the hollow between her breasts. Awai sighed and gave herself up to the constant sensations of heat then coolness, pain then pleasure.

It was a craft that Ty enjoyed, turning his future mate into a work of art. After he had dribbled lines of wax over her breasts, he created a trail down her belly, around the shooting star at her belly button, to her hairless mons. Ah, but he enjoyed seeing a woman so purely, so beautiful in all her splendor. He again tilted the candle and Awai gasped as he dripped the wax over the fullness of her mound.

Always he watched for signs of distress, waiting for what she called her "safe word." But Awai's expression was one of fear, anticipation, and bliss, constantly changing as he allowed the wax to coat her body.

When he had finished with the raspberry-scented wax, he used his magic to put out the fire on that candle and send it back to his table of implements. He then retrieved an ivory candle with an almond scent and started the process once again.

As he covered his mate in wax he could scent her increased arousal, could see it in the way she arched up to him and to the wax. So easy it would be to give in and to fuck her now. Never had he felt such raging desire that he could barely rein in his urge to take her hard and to take her now.

But no . . . she had much more to learn. And he had to take his time and give her the time she needed. If she could only trust him completely, all of those old chains would break, and his tigress would roar in ways she had only imagined.

Awai was amazed at how exciting it was to be coated in wax, as though her body was being coated in paraffin in the same manner her hands and feet were when she went to the health spa. But of course this was far more erotic. She had seen it done at the BDSM clubs, but it was something she had never experienced herself.

When Ty had finished putting a thick coating of wax from her breast to her mound, he put out the flame and sent away the candle with his magic.

Ty stepped back to survey his handiwork and smiled. Awai's dark hair splayed out against the white leather altar. Her pupils were dilated, her blue eyes focused on him, and her full lips slightly parted. Streaks of dark red candle wax mingled with pools of cooled white wax in swirling patterns. He had created a tunic of sorts over her naked flesh, but now he wanted to see what lay beneath it once again.

"A beautiful creation," he said, referring to Awai. By the skies he knew she had been created for him and him alone. He gripped the edge of the altar and leaned down to brush his lips across Awai's.

"Will you take me now, Majesty?" she murmured when

he withdrew. No doubt it would take but a few licks of his tongue against her clit and she would climax.

"No, slave." He shook his head, denying her once again. But his grip on the edge of the altar was so tight his fingers ached. Damnation, what this woman did to him!

Awai held her breath, staring in amazement as Ty gestured to the low ceiling and a large mirror seemed to melt through it. One moment it hadn't been there, and in the next she was staring at a large reflection of herself. She was spread wide, her wrists and ankles bound by the golden ropes, dribbles and drops of wax swirling over her body in the most unique patterns, unlike anything she'd seen in the clubs before. It was like she was a palette for Ty's work of art.

While she watched, he peeled off the wax in a single thick sheet that felt as supple as her thigh-high boots. The wax tugged a bit at her nipple charms, and around the star at her belly button, but otherwise it came off easily. Her skin felt smooth and pampered, and in the mirror very pink. Ty laid the wax art over a nearby leather-covered bar. When he turned back to her, he flicked one of his wrists and her bonds vanished.

While he helped her to a sitting position, Awai asked, "How do you do magic like that, Ty?" Realizing her error, she hurried to add, "Your Majesty."

Ty shook his head in slow motion and his frown indicated his disappointment in her. "Slave, you must learn not to ask questions out of turn. And you must learn not to refer to me by anything but Majesty unless I have given you leave to do so."

Awai lowered her eyes, her gaze landing on his huge cock outlined by his leather pants. "I am sorry, Your Majesty."

He hooked his finger under her chin and forced her to look at him. "This means I will have to punish you another time."

"But—" Awai bit her lip then said, "I understand, Majesty."

Ty assisted his little tigress down from the table, half wishing he could take her right now, and half pleased that he would be able to draw out her arousal until he made her so filled with desire for him that she would climax as she never had before.

Again using his magic, he retrieved a white satin blindfold. Awai gasped as he fastened it securely around her eyes, eliminating her sight completely. "There, my sweet," he murmured. "Now we are set for your third punishment."

He led her to a crystal bar, suspended with magic, just high enough that it would force Awai to hang with her hands over her head, and her feet would barely touch the ground. He strapped her wrists to each end of the bar, using the magical golden rope. When she was secured, he again used his magic to retrieve another spreader bar and rope, and knelt before her.

He paused for a moment, scenting her juices, wanting to taste what was there for the taking. Instead he forced himself to set about removing her white boots and tossing them aside. In moments she was completely naked, save for her collar, nipple rings, the charm at her belly button, and her blindfold.

She remained quiet, obviously fearing yet another punishment if she spoke out of turn. Ty smiled as he fastened her ankles to the crystal spreader bar. Anticipation would never feel so good as it would when he finally took Awai . . . for both of them.

While Ty strapped her wrists above her head, Awai trembled with excitement and fear as she hung in the air, visually blind to everything around her, but attuned to every touch, every sound, every smell. The scent of her own juices mingled with the raspberry and almond perfumes of the candles still on her skin. She caught Ty's male musk and the smell of the leather furnishing and equipment.

The air stirred and caressed her skin. The soft sounds of Ty binding her met her ears, as well as his boot steps as he moved from one side of her to the other. He teased her with gentle brushes of his skin against hers. God, what this man was doing to her. She had learned how to bring her subs to the very edge, but Ty had perfected the art.

His calloused palms secured her naked ankles to what had to be another spreader bar. He fastened her so that her feet were firmly on the bar that felt smooth and cool as glass. Once again she was spread eagle, only this time she was upright.

And then she was rising in the air. By the brief movement she could tell she only went up perhaps a foot above the marble floor. But it still was enough to make her heart pound just a little bit faster.

What was Ty going to do to her?

In the next moment she felt something freezing cold and wet on her buttocks and she realized it was ice. "How does that feel, tigress?" he murmured as he moved the ice down the crack of her ass.

Awai swallowed. "It feels amazing, Your Majesty."

But then he moved the ice to her pussy and she whimpered. It felt so cold against her clit. So cold it was like it was freezing her, yet burning her, too. She felt the brush of his heated skin as he moved around her, somehow keeping his hold on the ice cube. He moved it up to her mound, coating the bare area with the cold, cold moisture. In a slow movement he trailed the cube up her abdomen to her belly button, leaving it on her star charm for a moment until it was cold, too. Then he worked his way up the centerline of her belly to the area between her breasts. For a moment he simply circled each breast with the ice cube, but then he moved it to one nipple and pressed it tight.

Awai could almost feel her body heat melting away the ice, imprinting her nipple in its cold surface. The sensation was painful, yet a deep satisfying pleasure followed. Slowly he moved the cube to her other nipple, icing it in the same manner. Sharp pain shot from her nipple to her belly, then followed with a satisfying feeling.

Then the ice cube was gone and she held her breath, wondering what Ty would do to her next. Would he cane her or flog her? Maybe even spank her?

But the next thing she felt was a whisper-soft brush against her cheek . . . like a feather, yet not. Her heightened sense of smell told her it was something from the outdoors.

"Do you know what this is, my sweet?" Ty brushed her nose with the feathery thing again.

Awai caught her breath then said, "A leaf from a *ch'tok,* Majesty?"

"Yes." Ty brushed her cheeks with the leaf then slowly, lazily stroked it down her neck to her breast. "One of our most prized trees."

While Ty stroked and teased her body with the feathery leaf, Awai gave herself up to the sensations. He moved the leaf over her nipples and farther below. Awai found herself on a journey from the here and now, drifting into another time and place. As if she was traveling through the tunnel that had brought her from her own planet to this one. In that faraway place she thought of winter and holidays, summer and sailing, fall and pumpkins, spring and cherry blossoms. . . .

And then she was traveling back, back through time and space, back from the otherworld to find herself in the arms of her king, her Dom, her soon-to-be lover. Through a sort of haze she realized she was no longer bound or blindfolded, and he was sitting on one of the room's white leather couches, with her in his lap.

"Where were you, my love?" Ty murmured as he stroked her hair from her face in a gentle movement that belied the power and strength in the man.

"Subspace." The word came out as a whisper. Awai could hardly believe it. She had ended up slipping into what was known as "subspace" to those familiar with BDSM. Being a Domme, it was something she had never before experienced, although one of her subs had.

Ty smiled. "Wherever that might be, I am most pleased to have you back with me."

He leaned down and touched his mouth to hers, his kiss soft but his lips firm against hers. His long blond hair brushed her arm as he brought her tighter into his embrace and kissed her with far more intensity than he had ever kissed her before. He slipped his tongue between her lips, taking everything she had to offer, then drawing her tongue into his mouth and lightly sucking on it. When she moaned, he nipped at her bottom lip, lightly, then harder and harder until she was sure he would draw blood.

And she loved it.

She wanted to slide her fingers into his hair and pull him down and kiss him with all the intensity she felt in her soul. But she let him control everything that happened. He was the Dom and she had agreed to give herself up to him for his pleasure.

Was this what she'd been missing in life? Trying to prove that she was better than a man by being a Domme? She hadn't had to do that at all. She had proved herself through years of hard work in the corporate world, taking a man's world by storm.

But Awai Steele felt that part of herself separate from the woman inside. The woman who wanted to be loved and cherished.

The woman who enjoyed being Ty's submissive.

CHAPTER EIGHT

Ty pulled away from the kiss and studied his beautiful tigress. He tasted her on his tongue, smelled her desire and her unique scent. In more ways than he could count, he wanted her, desired her, needed her. She was like the blood in his veins, rushing through him and giving him life, fulfilling his destiny.

In ways that had pleased them both, he had punished her, had made her wait for him to fill her. But now he could wait no longer.

Ty stood in a fluid movement with Awai cradled in his arms. She gasped and clung to him as if he might drop her.

Giving her a firm look, he said, "Do you trust me, slave?"

Without pause, she replied, "Yes, Your Majesty."

"Then show that trust," he commanded.

Awai loosened her grip, sure he wouldn't drop her. Yet she couldn't help that out-of-control feeling that made her want to grab on to him again.

I do trust him, she reminded herself.

He carried her to a device that was A-framed like a sawhorse, only richly made, padded, and covered with white leather. Ty set her on it so that her chest, belly, and mound pressed to the padded crest of the A that was as wide as her hips. Her knees and arms rested on padded surfaces that were to either side of her, like shelves.

Awai shivered, wondering what he was going to do to her now. Would he fuck her like she wanted him to? Or would he make her wait longer?

Ty came around in front of her, and she saw that his face was a mask of concentration as he produced more golden rope. He hooked it through a loop she hadn't even seen, and before she knew it he had tied her wrist in front of her. Her pussy and breasts ached as her body pressed against the padded surface. In short order he had tied her other wrist, then was behind her where she could no longer see him.

"Are you ready, my lovely?" he asked as he trailed something rough down her spine, something that felt like the rope he'd used to bind her.

"Yes, Your Majesty." She was more ready for him than she wanted to admit. She wanted to scream, *Yes, damn it, fuck me now!*

But that would only get her more torturous waiting.

He trailed the rope over her back, down to her ass where he teased her, then moved it along the inside of her thigh, down to her knee, over her calf, and finally to her bare ankle where he proceeded to bind her.

It was all Awai could do not to scream her frustration.

She could feel her juices wet against the leather. Her nipples ached, the charms digging into her breasts as they were smashed against her chest.

By the time Ty had finished teasing her and had tied her other ankle, Awai was close to sobbing. She was on her hands and knees, her ass and pussy exposed to him. She was at the right height for his cock, and all he had to do was slide into her.

He caressed her butt cheeks with his palm. "What would you like me to do to you now, little tigress?"

"Fuck me." She sucked in her breath. "Please fuck me!"

"I am disappointed in you, slave," he replied in a cool, even tone. "You forgot your manners."

Shit. She dropped her forehead down to the padded surface and was tempted to bang it a few times. She raised her head up, and with as much remorse in her voice as she could muster, she said, "I am very sorry, Your Majesty. It will not happen again."

"Of course not." He continued to caress her ass. "But to ensure you learn your lesson, you must be punished. Do you understand?"

Shit shit shit. She was never going to get laid. "Yes, Your Majesty," she said through gritted teeth.

In the next second, Ty swatted her ass so hard she yelped in surprise and pain—not to mention it just about made her come. Again he spanked her as he said, "Do not climax or I will have to punish you far more severely than I have."

Ty spanked her ass again and again—first on one

cheek then the other, high then low, almost to the small of her back and down as far as her thighs. It turned Awai on so much that she squirmed to keep from coming. She clenched her teeth and dug her nails into her palms, doing everything she could to hold off the climax that was just at the edge. She was so close she had to bite her tongue.

Finally Ty stopped spanking her and her body went limp with relief that she'd made it, yet at the same time she was wound up inside so tight she might just explode.

Awai heard a whisper soft movement behind her and then Ty pressed something cool and hard to her anus.

"Do not climax until I give you permission, my sweet," he murmured as he pushed the lubricated device slowly up her ass.

It felt cold and smooth, like a glass cock. She'd enjoyed experimenting with various anal devices in the privacy of her home, even though she'd never allowed her subs to use them on her. She'd always been the one in control . . . or so she'd thought.

Ty pushed the crystal cock into Awai's ass, going slowly to make sure his mate was feeling nothing but pleasure. He also wanted to ensure she would be ready when he helped her fulfill what she had expressed as her greatest fantasy—to be pleasured by three men at once.

"How does that feel, slave?" Ty asked, surprised at how easily the thick crystal phallus slid into her.

He could tell it was difficult for her to speak by the breathiness of her voice. "It feels so good, Your Majesty."

Ty slid the crystal cock as deep as it could go and Awai gasped. "Have you used such devices before?" he asked.

"Yes, Majesty."

"Good. You will be prepared then."

Awai stilled, knowing that he was speaking of himself and the other two men fulfilling her fantasy. The thought excited and scared her all at once. What would it be like to be kissed and fondled by three men?

But she didn't have time to think anymore because Ty began sliding the glass cock in and out of her ass at the same time he slid two fingers into her pussy. "Would you like my cock now, Awai? Do you want me to fuck you?"

"Yes," she said, barely able to speak. "Yes, Your Majesty."

Ty slipped his fingers from her pussy but kept the glass cock in her ass. She felt the head of his cock at the entrance to her core and she almost whimpered, she wanted him so badly. "Beg me to fuck you," he demanded. "Beg me to punish you."

"Yes, fuck me!" she shouted. "Spank me, Majesty. I've been such a bad girl. Spank me while you fuck me."

He spanked her hard as he continued to fuck her ass with the crystal cock. Sweat rolled down Awai's forehead as she rocked back and forth, meeting each thrust of the device and each swat as he spanked her.

"Please, Majesty," she begged. "Please let me come."

"No." Ty drove the device harder into her ass and her butt stung from the swat that followed.

Awai tried to still, tried to keep her body from going over the edge, from reaching that point, but it was too much.

Her orgasm slammed into her and she cried out. She could do nothing but ride out the waves as he spanked her harder, and continued thrusting the phallus in and out of her ass.

Finally, when she was limp with exhaustion, he stopped. When he stepped into view his hands were empty and she knew he must have used his magic to get rid of the crystal cock.

He crossed his arms across his massive chest. "You disappoint me, slave. You have earned a severe punishment."

Crap. "I am sorry, Your Majesty."

With a wave, Ty released her bonds. "Come."

Awai crawled down, off what she now considered a freaking torture device. Yes, she'd had an incredible orgasm, but by the look on his face, she knew she wasn't going to like what he had in mind for her next.

Hopefully it involved fucking her, and soon.

He held out his palm and a circular length of golden rope appeared. "Hold out your hands."

Her pulse raced as she obeyed. Ty looped the rope around one of her wrists, then the other. When he was finished, her wrists were bound in front of her, so close that she couldn't move them.

"Follow me," he commanded and turned on his heel.

She followed, cool air brushing over her naked body. Her thighs were slick with her juices and tremors still rippled through her from her orgasm. When Ty reached the doors, he waited for her to follow.

His gaze held a challenge, as if daring her to argue over walking through his palace naked.

She raised her head and he looked satisfied as she followed him through the doorway. The tiles were cool under her feet while she followed him through the palace. They passed only Kalina on the way, and all the sorceress did was give the king a quick bow of her head before continuing on. She appeared to be distracted.

Which was fine by Awai.

By the time they reached their bedchamber, Awai was ready to do anything to please him so that he would fuck her.

Ty stopped before the round bed and faced her. "On your knees, slave."

With her hands still bound in front of her, Awai knelt in front of Ty. He flicked his fingers and his breeches and boots vanished, leaving only his beautiful naked body and that mouthwatering huge cock that she wanted inside her.

"I am going to fuck your mouth," he said in a growl. He grabbed her by the hair and dragged her toward his erection.

"Yes, Majesty." Awai parted her lips and Ty slid his cock through them, his fist still clenched in her hair.

Because her hands were still bound, she could do nothing but suck and flick her tongue along his length. She looked up at him and saw him watching as he thrust in and out of her mouth, pulling at her hair at the same time. Sweat gleamed on his chest and the club tattoo at his abs contracted as his eyes darkened.

Ty's cock stiffened and his thigh muscles clenched as he climaxed with a fierce growl. His fluid filled her mouth, sliding down her throat. He continued to pulsate and throb as he moved in and out a few times more, and then he pulled away.

Awai licked his come from her lips as she sat on her haunches and looked up at him.

"You will remain in your bedchamber until your punishment has been fulfilled," he said in an imperious tone that made her heart sink. "You will not wear clothing and you will not pleasure yourself."

Awai's bonds slackened, wide enough for her to use her hands, but she was still bound.

"If you attempt to bring yourself to climax, the ropes will tighten," he said. "If you behave, and do as you are instructed, I will come for you again."

Another wave of his hand and he was again clothed. "Do you understand why you are being punished, slave?"

Awai was tempted to shout *cherry blossoms,* but she nodded instead. This wasn't more than she could handle, was it?

"Yes, Majesty," she said. "I'm being punished for climaxing without your permission."

He nodded. "And the reason that is important?"

Grinding her teeth, Awai reached for an answer and found one faster than she expected. "Because I have to trust that you'll give me what I need, when I need it. That your pleasure will be mine."

Ty gave another quick nod. "Good. Servants will bring your food and prepare your bath. Use the time to think about whether or not you are willing to submit completely, to give over your pleasures and truly trust me. I offer only what you dream of, tigress. Believe that."

She was still kneeling on the floor when Ty strode past her and walked out of the room, shutting the doors behind him.

Slowly Awai got to her feet and walked to the bed, then threw herself facedown on the mattress. The nipple rings taunted her and her pussy ached. No doubt Ty's magical rope would keep her from taking care of matters for herself, but she needed to come again, so badly that she could just explode.

But he was denying her.

In order to fulfill her more completely . . .

Yeah, yeah, yeah. She knew the damned drill. She'd run it enough times, on the dominating side.

Was this what her subs felt? Helpless? Frustrated? Chagrined?

Turned on beyond all reason or imagination?

Damn.

But he was right. Damn again. Damn one hundred times.

If she trusted him, truly trusted him, she would find a way to deny herself until *he* thought the moment was right, until *he* would achieve the most pleasure. And therefore pleasure her all the more.

"This is fucking complicated." She moaned. Then she buried her face deep in the soft bedcover and screamed out all her pent-up sexual frustration until she was too tired to scream anymore.

* * *

During the day and a half that followed, Ty didn't come for Awai, which frustrated her to no end. If she even thought about touching her pussy, her bonds would tighten and she had no range of movement for the next hour or so. Two female servants had brought her meals and had helped her with her bath. Neither would speak to her, and Awai gave up attempting conversation with either of them.

After a time, she started finding ways to distract herself from her own physical needs. She would feel the pleasure building, building—the wants, the needs—and then she would just slip to the side of them, somehow. Into subspace. Into *her* space. Into a place where she had full power over her body, and never needed to fear or feel suspicious of a man again.

Today, the second morning, Awai sat upon the comfortable chaise lounge near the balcony doors. Sunshine spilled through the windows and warmed her naked body. She ached for Ty so badly that she did anything she could to keep her mind off of him, which wasn't easy. No matter what she did, her thoughts continued to stray back toward the man who she'd given herself up to as his sex slave.

Would being Ty's submissive truly allow her soul to be free as he thought it would?

Admittedly, the times when she could slip into that other emotional place made her feel strong, vibrant—powerful.

But, free?

More than once she'd considered shouting her safe word out the balcony doors, but she had chosen this role, and she was determined to see it through. At least until her nieces arrived.

She held a leather-bound book close to her chest, pressing it tight against her nipples, the charms digging into her flesh. She had just finished the book and felt a strange sort of discomfort, like something was wrong, but she couldn't quite place what it was.

While she'd waited for her punishment to end, she'd been spending her time sitting on the bed or the chaise lounge, reading books that she took from the beautiful bookcase hugging one curved wall. The books were fascinating, all with leather covers, the pages made of thick parchment, and the words written by hand. She took care as she read them, certain there could be very few of them in existence if Tarok didn't have printing presses.

The book she had just finished, the one in her arms, was the last book in the room on the history of Tarok. Awai had actually enjoyed her time reading. She'd learned about the centuries-old kingdom, including more recent times when the larger Kingdom of Tarok was divided into the lesser Kingdoms of Hearts, Spades, Diamonds, and Clubs.

To her surprise, Awai had also discovered that the brothers had a younger sister named Mikaela. She had left Tarok to wed Balin, the King of Malachad, one of Tarok's sworn enemies.

When Awai had read about the women of Tarok and

their inability to conceive, she understood the kings better and their need to find mates outside their world. They needed queens who would be immune to the mindspells of the Kingdom of Malachad.

Apparently Mikaela, now the Queen of Malachad, was believed to be the force behind the mind attacks. King Balin was thought to be under the queen's mind-control. Unfortunately the history book Awai had just finished left off at the point where the queen's treachery had been discovered by the sorceress and her cards. Perhaps books on more recent times were kept elsewhere in the palace.

While she read the history, Awai couldn't help but sense there was something missing—something darker and far more dangerous at play. She didn't understand the feelings, but they were there, perched on the edge of her consciousness, just out of reach. She had an image of herself, flicking her whip into that dark abyss, striking and pulling back what she needed to see and understand.

But her whip lay on her bedside table, unused for the last two days. Her bonds didn't allow whip practice. If they had, she might have slept better, but even her dreams had been haunted. Awai hugged the book tighter to her chest as she recalled the most recent nightmare she'd had. She'd dreamed she was the white tiger trapped in darkness at the end of a very long and black tunnel. Awai had floundered and fought to break free, but the darkness was too strong, too great to overcome, and she could do nothing to get away from it. Desperately, she cast about for an ally, a means of saving herself—but she found only emptiness and the doubling of the evil that held her fast.

Awai had woken before dawn, her skin coated in sweat.

"It must be these books that are getting to me," Awai murmured as she got up to put the book away. When she reached the bookcase, her bonds relaxed enough to allow her the movement necessary to place the history book back on the shelf. As soon as she finished, her bonds tightened again and she dropped them in front of her.

"Okay, I've learned my lesson," she muttered. "Now come and get me, Majesty."

The doors opened and Awai's gaze shot to them, hoping it was Ty. She tried not to show her disappointment when she saw that it was the sorceress instead.

Kalina smiled and gave a flick of her fingers. Awai's bonds fell away.

"You are free to roam the palace now," the sorceress said with a small bow.

"Thank god." Awai massaged her wrists. The ropes had never been tight enough to hurt her, but it felt good to know that she was free now. She grabbed a robe out of the wardrobe and slipped it on, tying it snugly at her waist. "Can I go anywhere?"

With a nod, Kalina said, "As long as you stay within the palace grounds."

Awai smiled and didn't wait. Maybe if she found Ty, he'd jump her now, she thought as she headed out the double doors. And then her smile turned into a small frown. No, likely he had a lot more teasing and torture in mind for her before he actually took her the way she desperately wanted him to.

CHAPTER NINE

Ty stood in the sorceress's chambers, his hands behind his back, his gaze focused on Kalina. Once she had given Awai permission to leave her bedchamber, the sorceress had met Ty in her own chambers.

Kalina now stood before the glowing *a'bin*, the table she used to predict the future of Tarok. She pushed her long fall of black hair over her shoulder, her fire-ice eyes studying the cards upon the table. These cards she used to tell the futures of Tarok and its four kingdoms, but on this day she had called him because the cards told a tale that she found both confusing and unnerving.

While he waited for the sorceress to interpret the cards, he glanced toward the lone window that was shadowed by heavy drapes. Kalina preferred her chambers to have little light save for countless candles perched upon every surface in the room. The smells of burning tallow, herbs, and perfumes filled the chamber. Amidst the plethora of scents, his keen weretiger senses caught her honeysuckle perfume, a scent that used to incite him, used to cause him to lust after the beautiful sorceress.

But now that he had found his mate, no one but Awai would ever do for him again. He had no desire to even look at any other woman. She was already ingrained in his heart and soul.

The king returned his gaze to Kalina, but her brows were furrowed in concentration and perhaps frustration, too. Ty moved to the window, his steps heavy in the silence. He pulled back the drape and smiled when he saw Awai seated by the pond, feeding the large, colorful fish with pellets of food provided by the gamekeeper. She looked so beautiful there, her hair in a shimmer of dark silk over one shoulder, her black robes clinging to her lush figure. He had missed her more than he wanted to admit, and it had taken all he had not to go to her last night.

"Majesty," came Kalina's musical voice, drawing him away from his view of Awai. He let the drapes fall back against the window with a soft swish as he turned to the sorceress.

He stepped closer to the sorceress's glowing *a'bin*. "What is it you read in the cards?"

She frowned, her forehead creasing as she gave another glance to the three rows of nine cards. "I see that our kingdom is in danger, but the cards are not telling me what that danger is." Her fire-ice eyes grew distant. "A tiger has been held captive for many years and is still imprisoned by a dark force."

Kalina raised her gaze to meet Ty's. "Perhaps your sister captured one of our people long ago and still lives to hold that weretiger captive."

He shook his head. "But I have seen the cliff where she met her doom. It would be impossible to survive such a fall." Even though his sister had turned to evil, he couldn't help but feel sorrow for the Mikaela he had grown up with and loved. "Her body must have been washed out to sea."

"You are probably right, Majesty." Kalina's lips pursed as she glanced again to the cards. "If that is the case, then we face a new threat." She glanced back to Ty. "And this force is darker and far more evil than Mikaela."

Ty studied the sorceress for a moment then gave a slow nod. "I will send word to my brothers and reinforce our own borders."

Even though he wanted to go to his mate, the safety of his kingdom and his people came first. He strode through the palace to the training yard where he knew his captain was working with new trainees. His mind worked over all the possibilities of the threat they faced. Could Mikaela have survived the fall? Surely her body would have been broken to bits by the jagged rocks below the cliff at Karn's Diamond Hall.

Despite the evil Mikaela had wrought upon all of Tarok, a part of Ty—that part of him who had loved his sister—felt hope that perhaps she did still live. Another part of him had hope that their kingdoms could return to normal and their women could once again bear children. Sadly, the two hopes could not be reconciled.

But if there were a way, if my sister yet lived and I could save her essence from the dark being she became, I would sacrifice almost everything to do just that. And I know Karn would do the same. Darronn is angrier, but no less loyal to Mikaela. Jarronn, though . . . I don't know if Jarronn has it in him to forgive our sister's many wrongs.

Ty paused when he reached the training yard to watch his captain sword-fighting with one of the newer recruits. The clang of metal upon metal rang through the air along with the curses and taunting of the captain as he jabbed at the trainee. The young man met each of the captain's blows with the skill of long practice and Ty smiled.

His thoughts turned back to Mikaela. If she had died, why then was the curse not broken? His brothers' mates had all borne children, but no other women in the four kingdoms had. Was it possible the mindspells had permanently damaged the minds of all of Tarok's women, keeping them from conceiving?

Can Mikaela still be alive, after all?

After speaking with his captain at length, and ensuring the kingdom would be well guarded, Ty sent messengers to his brothers with the sorceress's news. He did not, however, share his suspicions about Mikaela. It was better that each brother formed his own thoughts, for together, they would likely cover all possibilities.

When he was finished, he went in search of Awai. He shifted into a tiger and bounded toward the palace. He paused at the doors and scented the air. Yes, his mate had returned from outside.

With his magic he shoved open the doors and loped through, and then they slammed shut behind him. His paws made no sound upon the marble tiles while he followed the scent of his woman's musk to his private refuge, a hidden room he had never taken her to.

He eased into the room, his muscles rippling beneath his black-and-white striped coat, his eyes focused on the beautiful woman before him. The chamber was filled with family treasures, personal belongings, many of which he had had since he was a cub.

Sunlight filtered through the sheer curtains, highlighting Awai's dark hair. She had her hand at her throat as she studied the oil paintings of his family that his mother painted before she passed away. He caught the scent of fresh air and Awai's sweet perfume.

She reached out and touched the nameplate at the bottom of his sister's portrait. "Mikaela," she whispered.

Ty gave a low rumble and Awai startled.

"Don't scare me like that." She moved her hand to her chest, her heart pounding like mad. It was still unnerving to suddenly see a tiger beside her. "Please, Majesty," she added, not wanting to add to her list of punishments.

It was such an amazing sight to see him shift from tiger to man. Before her eyes he transformed, rising up on his hind legs as fur turned into skin and leather clothing, fierce tiger features giving way to a masculine face and long white-blond hair. In just moments he was the powerful man who had brought her into this world.

"I see you have found my sanctuary," he said, his expression impassive, not giving her any indication of how he felt about her stumbling upon this private room.

"Majesty, may I ask questions of you?" Awai asked. "May we drop formalities for now?"

He gave a slow nod. "Yes, my tigress."

Awai gestured toward the portrait labeled *Mikaela.* "I read a little bit about your sister in your history books. Why did she turn on you all?"

Ty's jaw tightened. "She was the youngest and for some reason our parents did not give her a portion of the greater Kingdom of Tarok. She resented that, and her resentment grew into a bleak mood that never departed. According to the sorceress's magical cards, Mikaela mind-seduced Balin, the King of Malachad, and became his queen. To seek vengeance on our parents, mostly. And on us, for holding a place in our parents' esteem that she evidently did not."

Awai turned to Ty. "The last book I found ended shortly after it was discovered she was behind the mind-spells. What's happened since then?"

"When our people could no longer bear children," Ty continued, "Kalina read the cards and learned that Mikaela was using powerful mindspells with our women, invading their dreams and making our women believe they are infertile."

He held his hands behind his back as he spoke, gazing only at the portrait. "When my brothers brought their mates to our world, she attacked, tried to harm each of the women."

Horror swept through Awai and her eyes widened as she realized he was talking about her nieces. "Did she hurt them?"

His gaze moved to hers and his eyes softened. "They were each injured, but not badly. You should be proud to know that your kin are such brave women."

Awai's mind whirled at the thought of Annie, Alice, and Alexi being in such danger. "Will Mikaela attack again? Is it possible that she could hurt them, or worse?"

Ty frowned. "We thought Mikaela to be dead. When she tried to harm Annie, Mikaela fell from a cliff to the rocks below. Her body should have been smashed, but when Karn searched for her, she was gone. He believed her body was swept out to sea."

Awai turned to the portrait of the beautiful woman with laughter in her blue eyes. It was so difficult to imagine her as evil and capable of harming anyone. "And now?"

A low rumble rose up in Ty's chest and she recognized it as frustration mingled with anger. "The sorceress believes we are in danger once again. She cannot discern if it is Mikaela or another dark force, but we must be prepared whatever the case."

He turned to Awai and brought her into his embrace. He smelled so good, and it felt so good to be in his arms. "My brothers will never allow harm to come to their mates. And I will never allow anyone to hurt you, my tigress."

She cocked an eyebrow at him. "Don't worry. I'm not helpless."

Ty took Awai by the hand and they walked through the palace, outdoors, and into the warm spring sunshine.

He enjoyed the feel of her small hand in his, her lithe body brushing against him. He needed to reestablish protocol, but he also wanted her to have something familiar to do, a part of her prior life, that would give her a sense of comfort.

When they reached a clearing in the cherry grove, Ty said, "Time for questions is over, and you must refer to me as Majesty."

Awai nodded and straightened her stance. "Yes, Your Majesty."

He held out his palm and with his magic called forth her whip and it appeared in his palm.

Her eyes widened. When he handed it to her a surprised expression crossed her face, but she took it without question.

Ty folded his arms across his chest. "I would like a demonstration of your skill with the whip."

Awai smiled as she grasped her whip. "Yes, Majesty."

They spent the next couple of hours with Awai displaying her talent with the whip and even teaching Ty a thing or two. He produced objects that she would snatch from his hand with a crack of her whip, the leather never touching him. He had never seen anyone so adept at handling a whip, save for his sister, Mikaela.

By the time they finished, Awai was laughing, her blue eyes sparkling and her cheeks flushed. He brought her close and her laughter faded as she stared up at him. The whip curled around their legs as if it had a mind of its own.

"You are so precious, tigress," he murmured and

brushed his lips over hers. "So very precious. Keep up your skills with your chosen weapon daily, at least two hours per day, without fail."

"Yes, Majesty," Awai murmured, and Ty could not help but kiss her again.

That evening, Awai waited for Ty inside the dungeon, her back to the doors, her hands behind her, and her stance wide. She was dressed in another miniscule white leather outfit. It had a tiny skirt and her chest was covered by a kind of strapless leather top, only there were holes where her breasts were, showing them to their full advantage. Her breasts were high and firm and the golden clubs dangled from her engorged nipples.

This time Kalina had massaged warm almond-scented oil into Awai's flesh after waxing her pussy. Awai always liked how it felt to have her mound and pussy lips waxed to feel soft and supple, and she knew that Ty loved it, too.

She shivered with anticipation as she waited for him. Likely he was taking his time, allowing her imagination to run wild, wondering what he would do to her. She was surprised at just how much she enjoyed her role as his sex slave, and how much she was looking forward to him coming for her now.

And she prayed that this time he would actually fuck her.

The moment he entered the dungeon, she sensed it with every fiber of her being. A gentle whooshing sound came from the doors opening and closing behind her, and a shiver trailed her spine as she heard the soft sound of paws coming toward her. Ty was in his tiger form.

He nudged her bottom with his large tiger head and she trembled. *Are you ready, tigress?* he murmured in thought-speak.

"Yes, Majesty," she said, her pussy growing even wetter with anticipation.

He sniffed and gave a rumble of approval. *Yes, my slave. You are indeed prepared for me. Do you wish me to fuck you now?*

Awai barely held back a moan. They hadn't even started and he was already torturing her with thoughts of him driving his cock into her core. "Yes, Your Majesty," she said. "I want you to fuck me."

Good. He padded around her and roared when he saw her naked breasts through her leather top. *You tease me, wench. You must be punished.*

She bit the inside of her lip as she looked down at the tiger and into his vivid blue eyes. He nudged the front of her tiny skirt, raising it slightly, then lapped at her folds with his rough tongue.

A cry escaped her throat and she barely remained standing, barely kept her hands behind her back. She wanted to grab his massive tiger head and hold him still, have him lap at her folds until he brought her to a fiery climax.

Ty growled his approval as Awai's pussy flooded with her sweet cream. He shifted, rising up to tower over her as a man. Her cheeks were flushed and her eyes dark with desire.

He palmed her breasts that protruded from the leather binding her chest. "Yes, you must pay for teasing me so." He pulled at her nipples, making the ache blend into a need so deep she could almost come from his touch upon her breasts. "Lie upon your back on the preparation table, slave," he ordered, pointing toward a white leather and mahogany table.

"Yes, Majesty." Awai visibly trembled with arousal as she obeyed him.

When she was flat on her back he commanded, "Raise your knees and spread your thighs."

He stood at the end of the table and smiled as he studied her lovely folds and her swollen clit. Within her line of sight, he held out his hand and called forth a clamp. He held it up for her to see and her eyes widened when she saw what it was.

Awai's excitement rose. She'd heard female subs say how much they enjoyed the feel of the clamp, but she hadn't tried it herself. And now Ty was looking at her with his intense gaze, holding it where she could see it. The clamp looked like a very short bobby pin with a golden club dangling from one end.

She swallowed as he lowered his hands toward her pussy. Her thighs trembled, waiting for that moment when he would clamp it over her clit.

He paused. "Do you wish to have my sign of ownership upon your beautiful quim?" he asked with one eyebrow raised.

Awai clenched her hands. "Whatever pleases you, Majesty."

"Make not a sound," he commanded, and in the next second he slid the clamp on her clit.

She gasped and arched her back at the intense pleasure. Amazingly there was no pain, just firm pressure that increased her lust.

Ty studied her for a moment. "I instructed you to remain quiet, slave, and you failed me."

"I am sorry, Majesty," she said, her voice trembling from the unusual sensations she was experiencing.

"More punishment is in order." He held out his hand and Awai grasped it, allowing him to pull her to her feet.

The club charm dangled against her pussy, stimulating more excitement as she walked. It was an incredibly sexy feeling as he led her across the dungeon to the corner where there was a cage with crystal bars. He gestured to the open door and said, "Get into the cage, slave."

CHAPTER TEN

AWAI'S HEART POUNDED AND HER MOUTH GREW dry. Was he going to lock her up and leave her? She knew he would do nothing to hurt her and she could always say her safe word. But would he hear her if she cried out to him?

When she hesitated, his voice came out in a low rumble. "Do you wish for me to add another punishment?"

She shook her head and knelt down on her hands and knees and crawled into the cage. The floor was a deep white carpet that was soft beneath her as she sat on it and looked up at him through the crystal bars.

He shut the cage door and waved his hand, and she heard the sound of a lock clicking into place. She sat up, her legs curled beside her and her hands in her lap.

Her pussy had a delicious ache from the clamp and she wondered if she touched her incredibly sensitive clit, how fast she would come.

As if hearing her thoughts, Ty said, "Raise your hands and grasp one of the bars above you."

"Yes, Majesty," Awai replied as she obeyed him.

Ty produced a length of the magical golden rope he so often used. He bound her wrists to the bar and then reached through the side bars and tightened each of her nipple rings. "Sit on your ass and spread your thighs, slave," he commanded when he finished.

Awai felt wanton and erotic as she obeyed. Her leather skirt climbed up to her waist and when she glanced down she saw that the top of her clit above the clamp was dark, engorged with blood. It looked and felt so sexy.

He rose to a standing position, stepped back, and smiled. "You make a lovely picture, my tigress. Perhaps I should have one of the court artists come and produce a portrait for me."

Her cheeks warmed at the thought of a strange man coming in and seeing her bound and helpless in the crystal cage.

"Would you like that, slave?" Ty asked.

Awai answered in the only way she could. "If it pleases you, Majesty."

He nodded. "It might." And then he pivoted on his booted heel and walked away, out through the dungeon doors.

In the quiet that followed, blood rushed in her ears. She quivered in anticipation and a bit of fear, wondering how long he would keep her locked up and if he truly would send someone to paint her portrait.

It seemed like hours before he returned, but in reality it was probably thirty minutes at best. Awai's arms ached and her nipples and clit were sensitized from the tightened rings and the clamp.

His boot steps echoed across the marble floor and her fear and excitement rose, one feeding off the other. When he reached the cage he propped his hands at his hips and stared down at her. She had to tilt her head back to see him. He looked magnificent with his long blond hair, broad tanned chest, black leather pants, and black lace-up boots. He was definitely a rogue of a man and she belonged to him.

With a magic wave of his hand he spelled away his clothing, leaving his gorgeous body entirely naked. He stroked his shaft, his eyes focused on Awai as he taunted her. "Do you wish to suck my cock? Or would you prefer to have me fuck you?"

Awai licked her dry lips. "I wish only for your pleasure, Majesty."

"On your knees, slave," Ty ordered, his voice rough, his eyes sparking with desire. "Come closer so that I might feel your mouth upon my cock."

"Yes, Majesty." The rope binding her wrists slid along the bar above her so that she easily reached him. He moved up to the cage, his cock thrusting toward her through the bars.

With her arms still tied above her head, Awai slid him into her mouth, all the way to the back of her throat. He gave a deep purr as he grasped her by her hair and began pumping in and out of her.

"You have a very talented mouth, slave," he murmured,

his voice deep and sexy. "Perhaps I shall just fuck your mouth and leave you here until the morrow."

Awai could say nothing, her mouth filled with his cock. She sucked him harder, more urgently, praying that he wouldn't leave her here. She could say her safe word, but she wanted him so badly she almost couldn't stand the ache.

He thrust in and out of her mouth, harder and faster. He was so big she knew he took care not to go too deep and not to hurt her.

Her breasts bounced and the clamp on her clit gave her such a delicious ache that she was afraid she would climax again and earn another punishment.

Ty's breathing grew ragged and he pulled his cock from her mouth. It glistened with moisture and was so incredibly large and hard. The head was purple and engorged, and veins stood out along the sides.

His voice was a low roar as he said, "Turn so that your back is to me and your ass against the bars."

It was a bit of a struggle with her wrists bound, but Awai was able to turn so that she was supported from the front by the rope ties, her ass against the bars. Her pussy was drenched with her excitement and she could smell her own desire.

Ty moved behind her and rubbed her ass through the bars. "Beautiful slave," he murmured. "You are mine to treasure, mine to command, and you are mine to fuck."

Awai moaned. God, she was so turned on she could scream. "I am yours, Majesty," she whispered.

He eased his hand into her slick folds and growled

his pleasure as he pulled at her clit clamp. With his free hand he reached through the bars and grabbed one of her breasts and tugged at the nipple ring.

She was so damn on the edge. "Please may I come, Majesty?" she cried as she pulled against her bonds, her body trembling with the effort to hold herself back.

"Not yet, slave." His rough tongue lapped at the soft skin of her ass, leaving a trail of warm moisture that cooled as he moved to another part of her buttocks.

Sweat was rolling down Awai's face in her effort to keep from climaxing. While he licked her ass, he continued to fondle her breast and play with her clit. The sensations were wild, unbelievable.

When Ty bit her ass she thought she was a goner from the sweet pain and pleasure of it. She managed—barely—to keep from falling over the edge.

"Very good." He released her clit and her nipple and grabbed her hips. Awai almost sobbed with relief as he placed the head of his cock against her pussy. The clamp on her clit was just short enough that he fit into her and she could experience both sensations at once.

"You are mine, slave," he said as he slid a fraction into her. "Tell me you are mine."

"I am yours, Majesty." Her words came out choked with need. "Do with me what you will. I am yours."

Ty gave a fierce growl as he grabbed her hips tighter and slammed his cock into her core. Awai screamed.

He was so thick, the length perfect. Filling her, driving to her center, pushing her excitement to levels she had never experienced.

She had known it would be good—but *this* good?

Damn!

All the sensations flooded her at once—the clit clamp, the tightened nipple rings, her bonds, the cold bars of the cage hard against her ass, and Ty's cock deep inside her pussy.

So right, so perfect.

Despite all her practice at controlling her body's reactions, she came almost at once, fireworks exploding in her mind and her cry echoing throughout the dungeon. Ty continued fucking her, slamming her ass against the bars, the pain unbelievably pleasurable.

Again and again she climaxed, but Ty didn't stop. He growled and roared and fucked her until stars filled her vision. *Is it possible to die from too much pleasure?* she wondered as another orgasm wracked her body.

This time Ty's roar shook the dungeon as he came, his fluid shooting into her core. He thrust several times more, then held her ass tight against the bars while his cock continued to throb inside her.

Awai sagged against her bonds, her body too boneless to move, too exhausted to think. Soft ripples of her last climax continued to roll through her as Ty slipped his cock out of her pussy.

"You came without permission, slave," he murmured. "I counted eight times. Shall we begin your punishment now?"

* * *

Awai sat beside a pool in the palace gardens, her legs curled up under her and one arm braced in the grass at her side while she watched the fish in the pool. They were beautiful and colorful, like everything else in this incredible world.

Her body ached in a sweetly used way and she never remembered feeling happier in her life.

In the weeks that followed that first time in the cage, Ty and Awai had spent more hours in the dungeon, and she found herself anticipating every new thing he did with her—from having her hang upside down while giving him a blowjob, to sex in a swing, and so many things she'd never dreamed anyone could do.

She had no doubt that Ty was always alert for any sign of distress or discomfort, but so far she had enjoyed everything he'd done with her.

I truly am a sub . . . but only for Ty.

In her heart she knew she could never be another man's submissive. But what did that mean?

Ty had also kept vigilant that she practiced with her whip at least two hours per day—and whenever else she wanted. He had expressed his amazement at her skill and had wanted her to teach him how to handle it as well as she did. He seemed both pleased and proud that she could manage such an unusual weapon—and relieved that she wouldn't be helpless if attacked by an enemy.

Though it's hard to imagine enemies in this lovely place. Or an enemy foolish enough to attack me when they'd have to answer to Ty.

It was such a new feeling, to be so sheltered and protected, so carefully tended and nurtured. Awai enjoyed being with her tiger-man, whether it was sex or spending time amongst his subjects, working out with her whip, or being alone, just the two of them spending quiet time together.

Awai picked a nugget of fish food out of a crystal bowl on the grass beside her. She tossed it at a large black fish with hot pink stripes. In one quick bite the fish swallowed the food and continued his peaceful swimming in the pond along with all the other brightly colored fish. They reminded her of koi, the large, colorful carp bred mostly in Japan for ornamental ponds and tanks. Yet like everything else in this world, these fish were different. More fins, larger eyes, more brilliant colors.

Beautiful, beautiful, beautiful.

The only thing that had marred her time in Tarok was the nightmares. That feeling of impending doom that she couldn't seem to shake. In the mornings she sometimes wanted to tell Ty about the dreams, but in the brightness of day they seemed surreal and trivial. What would she do, tell him she was having bad dreams? She wasn't a child, so why should she concern him with them? And that feeling of doom was probably just a part of her adjusting to a strange world and being concerned about all of her nieces.

Awai forced her thoughts away from the darkness of her dreams, and she easily turned back to thinking about Ty. It was like she couldn't get enough of him, as if she was addicted to him . . . his taste, his smell, his boyish grin, and the roguish glint in his blue eyes. His smell of musk and sun-warmed flesh and his teasing personality.

The way he held her in his arms when they went to bed each night. He'd hold her close, one leg hooked over her hip and his chest molded to hers. They both slept naked, and she loved the way their flesh melted together, the heat of his body seeping into her heart and soul.

Awai shivered and tossed another nugget into the tank, this time to a red, white, and blue fish that reminded her of the American flag.

All those years ago she had promised herself she wouldn't be dominated by any man. Yet here she was, a king's submissive.

A king who wanted her to be his queen.

But was that what she wanted? One of her self-made promises was that she would never get married again. And children? She wasn't sure she could handle one child, much less a litter like Alice and Alexi each had.

She still couldn't believe that. Might not believe it until she saw her nieces, which she could barely stand to wait for. And yet until the brothers felt like travel was safe, she would have to do just that—wait and wonder. And think about what to do with her life.

Besides, what about her career in San Francisco? Of course she had sold her business and had arranged for her wealth to be given to the women's shelter if she never returned. But again, did she want to stay in Tarok or return to the world she'd known and loved?

Or had she truly loved it?

Her life there was filled with memories . . . of her

brutal ex-husband, of her struggle to prove herself against men and to rise up on the ladder of success. Rung by rung she'd had to fight her way to the top and had trampled on a few men to get there.

Was that the kind of life she wanted, the type of person she truly wanted to be? Or had her bitterness driven her far beyond her heart's desires?

So many questions . . . and she wasn't sure she had the right answers.

Awai tossed a nugget at a green-and-purple spotted fish then turned her attention to all that was around her. This portion of the palace gardens was her favorite place to escape to. It was filled with cherry trees and their sweet smelling blossoms. Grass was soft beneath her robe and the breeze was just the right temperature. Not too cool and not too warm. It was a perfect spring day.

A few puffs of aqua-green clouds moved lazily across the sky, which was the same color as Alice's and Alexi's eyes.

Where are they right this moment? Awai brought her hand up and fingered her collar. *When will they arrive?*

"There you are, my tigress." Ty's deep voice brought Awai out of her thoughts and she tilted her head to see him standing beside her.

She dropped her hand from her collar to her lap. "Do you have need of me, Majesty?"

Ty crouched down beside her and gave her a cocky grin, his golden earring making him look even more like the rogue he was. "I always have need of you, my love."

Heat flushed over Awai, tightening her nipples beneath her robe and causing her clit to tingle.

He picked a nugget out of the crystal bowl and flung it in front of a large blue-and-black fish. "I've had word that my brothers are on the move. Our families shall arrive soon."

Delight and excitement filled Awai with such intensity she thought she'd burst. She moved her feet under her, sitting on her heels as she faced him. "When? I can't wait to see them!"

He gave her a frown but his eyes sparkled. "Must I punish you, Awai?"

Please do, she thought, but kept it to herself. "I'm sorry, Your Majesty. I'm so excited to see them that I forgot myself."

He gave a slow nod. "They will be here within two days."

Awai clapped her hands together, feeling like a giddy teen. She felt like laughing and crying all at once and her words tumbled out so fast she couldn't begin to stop them. "I've missed my family so much, Majesty. You just can't imagine what it means to me to—"

Ty caught her by her hair and pulled her roughly to him, kissing her with a fierce intensity that took her breath away . . . took all thought away.

When he released her, Awai could only stare at him, dazed and hungry with need.

He moved her so that she was lying on her back, staring up at him. With a gentleness that belied his strength, he pushed apart her robe so that she was entirely exposed to his gaze. All that she had on beneath the black silk was her collar and her nipple rings.

"You are the most beautiful thing I have ever seen," he murmured as he bent to brush his lips over hers.

"I love you, Awai." Ty cupped her chin and smiled. "And tomorrow, the day before our visitors arrive, I will give you the gift of fulfilling your deepest fantasy."

CHAPTER ELEVEN

Awai didn't know which statement to react to first. The fact that Ty had said he loved her . . .

Or that tomorrow would be the day she'd get fucked by three men at once.

She took the easiest—although perhaps it was the hardest—first.

"Cherry blossoms."

The invocation of the safe word seemed to startle Ty, but to his credit, he only nodded. The hard lines of control relaxed in his face, and he studied her simply as a lover and not as her Dom.

Awai sat up and clasped her robe tight around her, covering her bared flesh. "Don't say you love me, Ty." She felt right without the formalities of their protocol, because she didn't think this was time for play. It was too serious. "We've only known each other for a few weeks, and even though that's more than a month in Earth time, it's just too soon."

Ty moved his hand from her chin and slid his fingers into her dark hair. "I fell in love with you the very moment I saw your face in the card."

She frowned. "What card?"

"The sorceress's magical card." Ty wrapped his hand in Awai's long hair and brought it to his nose, inhaling the sweet scent of her cherry blossom shampoo. Still holding on to her hair, he moved his hand from her face and said, "You were all chosen by the fates. My brothers and I each chose a card . . . or rather the cards chose us. Whatever the reason, it brought you to me."

Awai's frown deepened. "I'm not too sure I like the idea of being chosen from a card."

"It was meant to be, my love." Ty released her hair as she rolled away from him and got to her feet, her back to him, gathering her robe more tightly around her slender frame.

With a sigh he stood and went to her, wrapping his arms around her waist. He held her back against his chest, and settled his chin on her shoulder. "What difference does it make how I found you, Awai?"

Ty's deep voice rolled through her and a part of her wanted to give in to his tenderness. But another part of her couldn't help but remember how charming and tender John Steele had been until after they were married. Would Ty change, too, if they were "joined"?

"You know I was hurt very badly once," Awai finally

said, determined to keep her voice from trembling. "I swore I would never fall in love again."

"Love is not something you fall into." Ty tightened his grip around her waist and snuggled closer to her neck. "Love is a feeling deep inside that says 'this is the one.' A feeling that cannot be denied, cannot be discarded simply because you have decided you will not love again. It is there forever."

"I'd like to believe you." Awai leaned her head back against Ty's shoulder and looked up at the aqua sky. "I thought I was so in love with John, but it was an illusion. I was in love with the man I thought John was, not who he really was."

"Exactly." Ty kissed the shell of her ear. "You were not in love with that bastard."

Awai turned around in his embrace, her eyes wide as she searched his. "What if you're an illusion, too? What if—what if—" She squeezed her eyes shut for a moment, trying to regain composure before opening them again. "What if you're not the man I think you are?"

Ty simply smiled and brought her hands to his chest and held them tight. "Listen to your heart, Awai. What does it tell you?"

So much emotion was flowing through her and she didn't know how to stop it. "My heart has been wrong before."

He shook his head. "I do not believe your heart fell in love with this man. He charmed you with gifts and promises. Not love."

Awai gripped his hands tight between them and pressed her cheek against his chest. His smell, the feel of his skin, the power in his embrace . . . everything about him seeped into her. She thought about his kindness to his people, how gentle and caring he could be, how he treated her with respect even when he was dominating her . . . all those things told her that he could be more than a lover and a friend, he could be her soul mate, one she was destined to be with, just like he had said.

"I need time," she murmured against his chest. "Please give me that."

Ty stroked Awai's hair as he held his tigress close. "You have all the time you need, my sweet. All the time you need."

She lifted her face, her eyes bright and a hesitant smile on her face. "May we go into the village again? I would like to buy gifts for my nieces." She frowned for a moment and bit the inside of her lip before saying, "I don't have any money. I've gone from wealth to poverty and I don't know how to deal with that."

He clenched her hands tighter to him. "Everything I have is yours."

When she shook her head, he released her hands and caught her face in his palms. "I took you from your world. I took you from everything that you knew and all your possessions. I give only what I have taken away." He gave that quirky, sexy grin that she liked so much. "Besides, I enjoy shopping for my nieces and nephews and my brothers' mates. Especially toys for the little ones. And since

Alexi is coming, I really should purchase a new cup to protect my ballocks . . ."

Awai laughed, feeling a little bit better about having nothing but the clothes she wore when she came to this world. In his deep blue eyes, Awai had seen that Ty meant everything he said, and somehow it comforted her.

He took her hand and led her through the trees filled with cherry blossoms and then down a long and winding stone path. The pathway was bordered by vines and bushes and trees unlike anything she'd ever seen before and she was still amazed by the beauty of it all.

The few times they had visited the village, Awai had been fascinated by everything she'd seen and experienced. Today was no exception. She again enjoyed looking at all the whitewashed buildings with brightly colored awnings and rooftops. The village smells of roasted meats, fresh baked breads, and clean fresh air wafted over her. They were comforting smells that made her feel at home, although she wasn't sure why.

Ty's subjects greeted them or smiled as they passed. Awai enjoyed watching the villagers exchanging pleasantries, going about their business, working in the various shops. She delighted in the magic that was used in their everyday life, from the baker summoning the yeast with her magic, to the fishmonger using a knife to fillet his fish without actually holding the knife; to the tailor using magic to sew a tunic; and the swordmaster folding the steel with her powers to make the finest of swords.

Ty took Awai to a toy store filled with magical toys:

colorful patchwork balls that disappeared at one end of the room and reappeared on the other side; a wooden village with wooden people that actually moved around on their own; fine porcelain dolls whose little faces scrunched up as they cried real tears, then their eyes brightened as they giggled with delight and clapped their hands.

Awai stared in amazement at all the wonderful toys. She didn't have any idea where to start, so Ty helped her by letting her know a little bit about the personalities of each child. Lance and Lexi were the oldest, being Alice and Jarronn's firstborn twins. Ty suggested finely crafted wooden toy swords as the pair liked to spar with each other, as well as with their father.

Then there were the five other girls: Puawai, who preferred toy warriors; Paula, who liked to play with toy elves; Karen, who favored toy villages and the wooden people; the toddler Jennifer, who liked dolls; and then there was Johanna, who was a year old and had a thing for whips.

"Like her aunt," Ty said with a smile. "Perhaps she will be a warrior like you."

Awai raised one eyebrow. "Like me?"

Ty nodded. "With your skills at the whip, you would easily be one of the kingdom's finest warriors."

Out of the four remaining boys, Tony was into knight sport; JB preferred intellectual games; Kyle wanted to learn about everything; and Matthew enjoyed anything he could build and tear down again.

By the time Ty had rattled off each child's age and what they liked, Awai's head was spinning. It was incredible how well he knew each child and their preferences, and she couldn't help but be touched by his love for them. And as he went through the store helping her select gifts, he was like a child himself, laughing and playing with the toys.

A joy Awai had never experienced before permeated her heart and soul. Could Ty truly be the man she would be willing to spend the rest of her life with?

Would she be willing to spend the rest of her life in this very different world?

After they finished buying toys for the children, Ty paid for the items and had them all sent to the palace. They continued shopping, Ty helping Awai choose what was unique to his village that he was certain the three queens would not already have. One of the things his village specialized in was extremely prized handblown glass. For her nieces, Awai chose beautiful vanity jars, in purple, blue, and pink.

For the kings she was at a loss, but Ty took her to a fine leather shop where they ordered three specially made dagger sheathes, one with a heart, the second with a spade, and the third with a diamond, each symbol made from the finest gold filigree and precious gems.

As they shopped, Ty bought a basket and filled it with foods from the various shops, including breads, meats, cheeses, *alnea* fruit, ale, and Awai's favorite cherry tarts. Ty enjoyed supporting his people in their endeavors, and always paid a little extra for whatever he purchased.

When they finished shopping, Ty took Awai to the lake that lay to the east of the village. They chose one of his sailboats from the dock, a black one with a gold club emblem on its side and golden sails. He watched the delight on Awai's face as they sailed on the peaceful green water. It was so clear they could see fish swimming close to the boat, and the brightly colored plants waving from where they were rooted in the clay below. Awai's dark hair blew across her cheeks in the breeze, her blue eyes sparkled, and a smile curved her full lips. She was so beautiful that Ty's heart ached just looking at her.

He didn't want to share her on the morrow with his brothers-at-arms. It was killing him to even think about it, but he had promised to fulfill Awai's fantasy.

After they finished eating the meal Ty had bought in the village, they relaxed on the deck of the sailboat. Awai positioned herself between Ty's legs, her back to his chest, her head resting against his shoulder, and he wrapped his arms around her waist.

She felt so comfortable, so cared for that she wanted that moment to last forever. Water lapped at the side of the boat and in the distance she thought she heard a wolf's howl. A cool wind chilled her cheeks and caused her nipples to stand out even tighter against the black silk of her robe. Fresh air, pine, and other scents she couldn't identify mingled with Ty's earthy smell that surrounded her, comforted her.

Aqua clouds were backed by purple and bright pink streamers that streaked across the blue-green sky. Bits of gold glittered in the air like confetti, reminding her of New Year's Eve at the grandest of balls in San Francisco. "Just look at that sunset," she said. "I've never seen anything so beautiful."

"I have." Ty held her closer and nuzzled his face in her hair. "You are the loveliest thing in our world that I have ever seen."

Awai smiled and snuggled closer to Ty. With him she knew that his comment was sincere, not just flattery. She could feel his erection pressed up against her backside, yet he didn't ask for more than just holding her. They both had been content to spend time with one another today, but now she wanted him, wanted to feel him deep inside her.

She tilted her head up so that she could see Ty's face. His strong jaw, the intense look in his blue eyes, his blond hair stirring in the breeze. He leaned down and captured her lips in a breathtaking kiss that left her feeling as though she'd never be able to breathe on her own again.

In one of his smooth, lithe movements that caught her off guard, Ty shifted them both so that he was lying on the deck and she was on his chest, her hands braced on the deck to either side of him. She never wore underwear, so beneath her robe her bare pussy was against his leather-clothed cock. Her hair fell to either side of her face as she stared down at him. "If I get to be on top this time, does this mean you'll call me Mistress?" she teased.

Ty gave her a mock frown but even in the waning light, she could see the roguish glint in his eyes. "I believe that earns you a punishment, tigress."

Awai gave him a small pout. "What can I do to make up for my misbehavior, Your Majesty?"

He reached up and pulled apart her robe so that her breasts were bared to him and the evening air. With little effort, Ty pushed the robe down her arms so that it fell from her body, and she was completely naked astride him. Awai arched her back, thrusting her breasts forward, offering them to her god of a man. He palmed them, massaging them as she rubbed her clit against his erection.

"I know exactly what you can do to pay for being so impertinent." He pushed her down a bit so that she was on his thighs and then he freed his cock from his breeches.

"Suck my cock, woman," he demanded with that glint in his eyes that Awai found irresistible.

"Yes, Majesty," she murmured as she wrapped her fingers around the girth of his erection. She brought her mouth to the head of his cock and swirled her tongue over the head. Ty groaned and Awai gave a satisfied smile before she slid her lips over his shaft and took him deep within her mouth, far enough that his cock touched the back of her throat.

"That's it, slave." Ty grabbed handfuls of her hair as she worked his cock with her mouth and hand.

Awai loved the way it felt when he tugged on her hair, forcing her up and down while she sucked his cock. It hurt so damn good.

"Without stopping," he said, "I want you to move so that your quim is over my face so that I may lick your clit."

Awai's pussy ached at the thought. She kept her hold and her mouth on Ty's erection while she moved so that her slit was directly above his mouth and they were in a sixty-nine position.

The moment she was over him, Ty said, "Do not stop

sucking my cock for any reason, and do not climax without my permission."

He parted her folds and licked her from her clit all the way to that sensitive area between her core and anus. Awai almost paused, but managed to keep going, using swirling motions and lightly scraping her teeth along his length just to get even with him for what he was doing to her.

But when he stuck two fingers into her core and sucked on her clit, all thought abandoned Awai's mind. She went still, fighting off the orgasm that was racing toward her like a freight train.

Ty reached up and smacked her ass cheek hard with the flat of his hand. Awai lost it. Her orgasm roared through her so fast there was no way she could stop from coming. Ty kept sucking and licking and spanking her, driving her beyond sanity.

When she could take no more, she let his cock slide from his mouth. "Please, Majesty, stop."

"You have earned two punishments." Ty moved Awai so that her ass was on his chest and she was sitting up. "Stand and go to the rail. Bend over and brace your hands on the rail and keep your stance wide."

Awai obeyed, a thrill skipping through her body at the thought of what Ty was going to do to her.

Instead of fading, the sunset was more incredible than before. It was like the aurora borealis, with misty, shifting colors that hung like iridescent curtains of light from the sky. The sails of the boat glowed as if on fire, as if feeding from the cosmic light show. The aurora spanned the sky as Awai bent over, her hands braced on the railing of the black sailboat, waiting to take her punishment.

Ty took his time, increasing her anticipation by making her wait. Cool air caressed her slit from her clit all the way back to her ass. She imagined him flogging her, or perhaps spanking her until she was so close to coming she would beg for mercy.

The golden clubs dangled from her nipples and her shooting-star charm swung from her belly button. Every movement against her body, every sway of the boat, every flap of the sails, every shift in the sunset's light show—it was all about to drive her out of her mind. She wanted the waiting to be over, yet she didn't want it all to end. It was one of the most intense experiences she'd had.

Awai sensed when Ty was finally behind her. It was a sixth sense, a way of knowing that her man was close.

The thought more than gave her pause.

My man.

Before Awai could explore the concept any further, Ty pressed his completely naked body against hers. She could feel his cock against her tailbone, the soft curls around his balls caressing her ass, the light coating of hair on his legs brushing against hers. He put his hands on her hips and bent closer so that his muscular chest was pressed to her back.

"Who do you belong to, Awai?" he murmured as he nuzzled her hair.

"I—I belong to you, Majesty," Awai replied, then stilled as she realized she meant it.

She belonged to Ty . . . body, soul, and heart.

Her whole body went weak at the knowledge. She was in love with Ty.

"That's right, my sweet," Ty was saying, bringing her out of her stunned state of mind. "You belong to me . . . always."

Awai wanted to say *yes, always,* but she was too overwhelmed by the feelings in her heart and soul.

She was in such a daze that at first she didn't realize he'd moved around so that he was near her face. She missed the feel of him pressed to her back, but his cock was so close to her now that she was mesmerized by the sight of it. It was amazing to her, how much she enjoyed going down on him, having him inside her in any way he could possibly take her.

One of his golden ropes glittered in his hand and then he tied her wrists to the boat railing. "Now you're going to finish sucking my cock," he said as he grabbed a handful of her hair the way she liked it and moved his erection to her lips. Awai sighed as he filled her and began fucking her mouth with slow, deliberate strokes. She closed her eyes and concentrated on applying suction at the same time she swirled her tongue along his length.

A rope slapped her ass, hard, causing her eyes to pop open. The brief pain felt so good that she was on the verge of climaxing yet again. Lash after lash of the golden rope landed on her backside, drawing her closer to the brink, yet the strikes were varied enough to keep her from going over the edge.

His body tensed and she knew he was on the verge of

climaxing. She sucked harder and at the same time she hummed.

Ty's roar filled the night as he came, his seed pumping down Awai's throat.

CHAPTER TWELVE

THE SOUND OF TY'S TIGER ROAR ECHOED FROM one end of the lake to the other as he came, and Awai imagined all the people in the village and palace watching her and Ty. The thought of being watched was almost more than she could handle, and she was so close to coming she could have screamed if it wasn't for Ty's cock still in her mouth. It still felt firm and huge, even as she milked the last of his semen from it.

"Enough!" Ty shouted as he pulled his wet staff from Awai's warm mouth. If she did not stop, he was sure he would come yet again and he wanted to fuck her more than anything.

He moved around behind her and rubbed her ass with his palms and then spanked her. She cried out, and even as her cry carried on the night wind, he thrust his cock into her quim, burying himself in her silky heat.

Awai couldn't believe how this moment could be even

more exciting than all the time they'd spent in his dungeon, trying out every device he owned. No, there was something about this night that went beyond sex.

Ty moved his cock in and out of her channel, his hands gripping her hips. She tugged against her bonds as she tried to press herself harder against him. "Please let me come, Majesty," she begged.

"Hold, tigress," he commanded as he drove into her harder, his balls slapping against her pussy.

Awai bit down on her lip, hard enough to draw blood, as she fought off her orgasm. The coppery taste flowed over her tongue and a buzzing sensation took hold of her body. The evening's light show faded as she became completely lost to the sensations filling and surrounding her. She had improved in her abilities to manage her body. Somehow, she held back, and held back, and held back . . .

"Climax for me, tigress!" Ty shouted.

Awai released her hold on her lip and cried out with relief and with ecstasy as her whole body shook with her orgasm. The colors of the aurora swirled within her vision and they seemed to sing in tune with her climax. Her knees trembled and she sagged against her bonds as the world gradually came back into focus. Ty kept his grip on her hips and growled as he came again.

With his magic, Ty released the bonds from Awai's wrists. At the same time he used his powers to retrieve a thick cushion from belowdecks and lowered himself and Awai to it. They lay cuddled together, her back to his chest, her firm ass nestled against his cock.

For a long while they watched the light show overhead, the rare *banuk* that came and went without explanation. He gently stroked her hair from her face and she gave a contented sigh that made him smile. Water lapped against the side of the boat and a night bird's song blended with the *banuk*.

Awai sighed again, so happy that she didn't think she could stand to be any happier. She wanted to tell Ty of her revelation, but something kept her from it. She couldn't quite place her finger on what it was, but it was like one more piece from a work of art had yet to be completed. Perhaps it was that she wasn't sure about leaving her home, her life, her career permanently. Perhaps it was because of her scarred heart.

Instead of worrying about the reasons any longer, she relaxed against Ty, enjoying the magical night and wishing it would never end.

Late into the night, Ty docked the sailboat and after using his magic to clothe them both, he carried his sleeping mate to the palace. He tucked Awai into his bed, covering her with a thick blanket and brushed his lips across her brow.

Even as he turned away, he shifted into a tiger and bounded from the room. Frustration seared his veins like molten fire and roared in his head like the most powerful of storms. He tore through the palace and out into the forest, running with no other purpose than to work through the most difficult situation he had ever had to face as a king or as a man.

For hours he loped through the trees, straying from winding paths into the wilds, his mind filled with what was to come on the morrow. How could he share his woman with two other men? Yet how could he take away the opportunity to make her happy by fulfilling her fantasy? He could tell her she was no longer allowed her dream, but then she might hate him for taking away something that was important to her.

He damned himself for letting the men touch her, for giving her the choice to begin with. But that's what it came down to . . . Awai's choice.

Ty's roar echoed through the hills, sounding desperate even to his own ears.

Darkness fell like a cloak over the white tiger, melding with the beast until they were as one.

Awai backed away from the darkness and stumbled over her whip. She scooped it up and faced the dark void that threatened to swallow her. Small cries came from all around her. She had to protect them, had to keep the darkness away . . .

Awai woke to find the covers twisted around her body and her skin damp with sweat, and that she was alone. "Why am I having these dreams?" she whispered to the ceiling. Was her consciousness battling with her over Ty—was he the tiger in the dream?

No. There was no doubt in her mind that Ty was a good man. Through his domination of her, he had freed her mind and her soul. And maybe even her heart.

But she felt an unexpected emptiness in her heart

and soul. After the beautiful night they'd shared, she couldn't understand why she felt such an ache, such a void.

And today was the day she would have her wildest fantasy fulfilled.

Three men.

At one time.

Her motions through the entire morning were automatic, her mind on Ty and what was to come.

Awai had no hunger for the breakfast that was brought by palace servants. She played with her food, pushing the strange-colored fruits around the plate, arranging them in patterns that reminded her of the sunset light show last night. Instead of the feeling of joy she'd had last night, lead settled in her belly.

What's wrong with me? She'd just had the most incredible night with a man she'd fallen for, and now he was going to fulfill her fantasy by sharing her with two other men.

Her fork clattered on her plate at the thought. *Ty. Me. Two other men.*

She turned her thoughts away and stared instead outside. It was a dark and gloomy day, like a storm rode the skies. In the distance she saw flashes of lightning and raindrops began pelting the windows in quarter-sized drops.

Kalina swept into the room. The sorceress was a dark-haired goddess whose beauty and charm only made Awai feel more unsettled.

While she helped Awai bathe, the sorceress remained quiet, as though sensing Awai's inner turmoil. Afterward

Kalina prepared Awai to go to Ty . . . and Kir . . . and Rafe.

Awai's stomach clenched and she couldn't wrap her mind around what she was about to do. The first time she'd gone to a BDSM club she'd been nervous, but nothing compared to how this made her feel.

It's just nerves, she told herself.

No. It was something more, something far more than just being nervous or having second thoughts.

Awai allowed herself to be escorted to the dungeon, and then Kalina left her outside the double doors. The white leather dress she was wearing felt too small, too skimpy, too flesh-baring. But that was the idea. She was supposed to turn on three men, all at one time.

She took a deep breath and pushed open one door and slipped into the dungeon. The door banged shut behind her like a concrete lid sealing a tomb. It was dimmer than usual, with candles flickering around the room, and she had to blink until her eyes adjusted.

Her breath caught as her gaze rested on Kir and Rafe. Kir stood with his arms crossing his massive chest, and Rafe had one shoulder hitched against the wall as he studied her with obsidian eyes. They both wore leather breeches and boots, but both had bare chests that any red-blooded woman would want to rub her hands over.

Where's Ty?

"Are you ready, milady?" Kir said with a lazy sort of drawl to his voice.

Rafe just watched her with his dark gaze, as though seeing into her soul, seeing something that she didn't.

It came to Awai then. No, she wasn't ready. She'd never be ready. She wanted Ty and Ty only.

And what had been upsetting her so badly had been the fact that Ty would be willing to share her in any form. *How can he love me if he'll let other men touch me?*

The dungeon doors swung open and a white tiger bounded through with a roar that rattled windowpanes and snuffed candles. He came to a stop then stalked slowly toward Kir and Rafe.

Neither man moved or seemed the least bit concerned. The tiger gave another room-shaking roar and then shifted . . . into Ty.

He stood with his back to Awai, facing the two men. "I will not share this woman," he growled. "She is my heart, my soul, and she belongs to me."

Awai's own heart began pounding in her throat and the joy that had been missing all morning suddenly filled her again.

Kir bowed and Rafe looked amused. "It is as I expected," Kir said. "She is your lifemate and I must say it took you long enough to realize you could not let us have her in any way."

Before Awai had time to blink, both men shifted into wolves. The golden wolf gave a quick howl, then both loped from the room. If she didn't know better, she would have thought the two of them were laughing.

Ty slowly turned to face Awai, his chin high, his hands clenched into fists at his sides. "I am sorry, Awai. I tried to fulfill your fantasy, but I could not. I love you, and I can never share you with any man or woman."

Awai ran toward Ty and jumped up, grabbing him around the neck and wrapping her legs around his waist. She pressed her lips to his, kissing him long and hard. He buried one hand in her hair while his other hand cupped her ass, holding her tight.

When she pulled away, Ty stared at her with a shocked look. "You are not angry with me?"

She shook her head, her hair sliding across her shoulders and onto Ty's chest. "I can't be with anyone else. I realized that today." Her eyes locked with his as she added, "You don't know how happy it makes me that you feel the same way."

The relief that rushed through Ty was so great that he gripped Awai tighter to him as he gazed into her beautiful blue eyes. "Are you sure, my love? I feared you would be disappointed with me for not giving you your fantasy. But I can never allow another man to touch you."

Awai smiled. "I love you, Ty, and you're the only man I'll ever want or need."

Ty let loose with a roar, then kissed her long and hard, letting her feel all the pent-up frustration and joy he felt at that moment. He held her close while he strode through the still open doors. With his magic he slammed the doors shut behind them as he carried Awai from the dungeon and through the palace. She kept her legs locked around his waist, her arms around his neck. Her smile was radiant and he could see the love in her eyes that matched his own.

While he strode through the palace, intense joy flowed through his heart and soul. Awai had declared her love for him and he wished to shout it out so that all might hear.

When he reached his bedchamber he carried her straight to his bed, straight to the one place he wanted to keep her forever. With a flick of his wrist he lit candles scattered across the room, bringing light to what was dark from the storm outside.

He laid her gently upon the soft coverings and she released her hold on him. For a moment they stared at each other in silence. She looked so beautiful, her dark hair splayed out behind her, the white leather dress hugging her slender body, her breasts ready to burst from their bonds.

She held her arms out to him. "I want you. I need you. No roles, no playing."

He smiled at her and lowered himself onto the bed beside his woman. He wanted to love her like he never had before, and then he wanted to show her that she was his in every way imaginable.

Awai sighed as Ty lowered his lips to hers. Gone was all the doubt and indecision. She knew he would never harm her in any way.

He would love her and protect her always, and she would do the same for him.

Ty pressed his length along hers, rubbing his leather-clad cock against her hip. Slowly he pushed aside one of the straps binding her breasts, freeing it. He leaned down and flicked his tongue over the nipple and the club charm, and then he gently blew air upon it.

Awai gasped and arched toward him, but he moved to

her other breast. He pulled aside the leather strap and released her breast from its confines. This time he suckled her nipple before blowing air over it and the heat between her thighs grew more intense than ever before.

"Fuck me, Ty," she begged. "I need you to thrust so deep I feel it in the back of my throat."

Ty shook his head. "Ask me to make love to you. After we make love, then I will fuck you."

"You're not making sense." Awai placed her hands on his muscled chest. "No matter how we do it, I want you and you want me."

"If you don't know the difference, my little tigress, I have been lax in my teachings." Ty brought his hand to Awai's face and rubbed his thumb in a whisper caress over her lips. "This is not about driving my cock into your core." He skimmed his fingers along her jaw and smiled. "It is about showing you my love in how I touch you, feel you."

Awai trembled in response to Ty's touch and her heart ached at his words. To truly be loved was something she'd never expected to happen. Even though he had told her, now he was showing her what he'd meant.

Ty gently undressed her, easing the straps of her dress from her shoulders and down to her waist. He rose from the bed and slid the leather outfit from her hips, down her legs and feet and then tossed it aside. Every move he made was slow and sensuous.

When Ty finished undressing Awai, he looked at her and sucked in his breath. His woman was so beautiful she caused his heart to ache and made it hard to breathe.

For a moment he simply swept his gaze over her body. From her dark chestnut hair to her full, beautiful breasts, to her hairless mound, and shapely legs, then back to her blue eyes. She wore nothing but his collar and nipple rings and the star charm at her navel.

"Words cannot be said to express how beautiful you are, my love." Ty held out his hands in a helpless gesture. "From your heart to your soul to your body, you are beautiful."

Awai bit her lower lip, afraid she was going to cry. The moment was so precious with Ty's love so clearly expressed. "How did I get so lucky by finding you, Ty?"

He smiled. "I found you."

She returned his smile and started to get up, to go to him, but he shook his head and said, "No, stay there where I might watch you as I undress."

Instead of spelling away his clothes with his magic as he had so many times before, Ty removed them himself. He flexed his broad, naked chest then raised his foot to the bed and unlaced one boot as he watched her intently. When it was undone he brought up his other foot and unlaced his boot. He stood and kicked both boots away so that he was standing on his bare feet.

The entire time Ty kept his gaze focused on Awai. Wetness seeped between her thighs and she ached to hold him, to love him. But his movements were slow and purposeful as if to make this moment last an eternity.

It surprised her how much she wanted this. How much she wanted to hold this moment in her mind's eye, to remember every word, every movement, every touch.

"I am going to taste every bit of your body," Ty promised as he undid his breeches. "I intend to lick the salt from your skin, to taste the cream from between your thighs. To show you my love in every possible way."

Awai squeezed her thighs together, trying to ease the ache that his words caused. But he shook his head.

"No," he said. "I want your legs splayed wide so that I might view all of you."

She spread her thighs, showing him her swollen folds and her clit that ached for his hands, his tongue, his cock.

A rumbling rose up in Ty's chest and she sensed that he was on the fine edge of control.

Awai lowered her eyelids. "Let me see all of *you*."

He widened the opening of his leather pants and his cock sprung free. Awai ran her tongue along her lower lip, wanting to taste him. But he took his time, sliding his pants down over his tapered hips, muscled thighs, and powerful calves, until he was naked.

She sighed. What a beautiful man, inside and out. He stood there watching her, his head high and proud, his white-blond hair flowing past his shoulders, his muscles straining with the force it took to hold himself back. She could see that restraint in his eyes, could sense it in his very presence.

"Come to me," she murmured, beckoning him with her hand and her eyes. "I want to make love to you."

Ty had never wanted Awai more. Knowing that he had won her love was a powerful aphrodisiac that made his fine rein of control tenuous at best. He forced himself to move closer to the bed. She went to reach for his cock but he shook his head. This was her turn to be pleasured in every way that he could.

He eased onto the bed so that they were lying face to face, their bodies inches apart but the heat of her body melding into his own. He brought his hand to her cheek, her skin soft beneath his calloused fingertips. Gently he slid his hand to her lips and she parted them and flicked her tongue over his index finger.

Ty's breath hissed as she sucked on his finger and he imagined her going down on his cock. But he continued his movements, trailing his wet finger over her chin, down to the hollow of her throat, and between her breasts where he could feel her heart beating a rapid rhythm.

"I scent your arousal," he said as he explored her breasts, feeling the weight of one in his hand and then the other. "I can hear your heart beating for me." He squeezed her nipples, feeling the taut nubs tighten even more beneath his touch.

"I can't wait." Awai brought her hand to his stubbled cheek that felt coarse as sandpaper against the soft pads of her fingers. "I need you now."

With a shake of his head, Ty refused her. "This is about making love, Awai. Not fucking. When I take you tonight, you will know that you are mine and I am yours."

"I understand that now." A moan escaped her throat as Ty dipped his head and licked the nipple he was still squeezing. "But you're driving me crazy."

Ty raised his head and gave a soft laugh. "I have only just begun."

CHAPTER THIRTEEN

TY CUPPED HIS PALM AND TO AWAI'S SURPRISE, A handful of cherry blossoms appeared. He sprinkled the blossoms over her hair and down her shoulder to the curve at her waist and hip. When he had a single bloom left, he brought it to her face and feathered it across her cheek.

"The petal smells wonderful and is so soft." She sighed at the erotic feel of the bloom. "Yet your touch leaves a path of fire behind."

"Your skin is silkier and fairer than this blossom." Ty slid the petals from her cheek, over her lips. "And your scent is far more beautiful."

Awai trembled at the sensual teasing as he trailed the bloom along her jawline to her ear. The ache between her thighs grew and she could smell her own arousal mixed with cherry blossoms and Ty's scent—the smell of a clean breeze on a spring morning blended with an intoxicating musk of man and weretiger. They were still both on their sides, facing one another, and she longed to reach out to him, to touch him the way he was touching her.

Candleflame and shadow flickered over Awai's features and Ty smiled at the beauty of it. She reached for his cock, as if to stroke it, but he shook his head. "Not yet." He brought the bloom to the hollow of her throat and let it rest there for a moment. Cherry blossoms were white and pink jewels against her dark hair and her dark lashes made crescents against her skin as she surrendered to him.

She tilted her head back, closing her eyes and fully exposing her throat to him. Whether or not she realized it, in his species that was a sign of total submission and complete trust.

He lowered and kissed her throat below her black collar, lightly flicking his tongue over her pulse point and tasting her skin. When he drew away, he brought the bloom over the curve of her breast, then teased her nipple into an even tighter peak. He loved seeing his sign of ownership upon his mate—the collar and the nipple charms.

"Lay upon your back," he murmured as he gently guided her.

When she was on her back, she opened her eyes and gazed at him. He called forth more cherry blossoms and sprinkled them over her full breasts and flat belly, and onto her mons. Awai's lips parted and her chest rose and fell as she took a deep, shuddering breath. Blooms slid down her breasts and onto the bedcovers.

Ty picked up two blooms that had fallen to the bed and brushed the twin blossoms over one of Awai's nipples as he dipped his head and tasted the nipple closest to him. He flicked his tongue over the taut nub and the dangling club charm.

Awai gave a whimper. "I didn't know men like you existed."

A growl rose up in Ty's throat at the thought of any other man being with his woman. "For you I am the only man who exists."

"Only you," Awai said as she reached out to brush his hair away from his face. "You're my man as much as I'm your woman."

Ty purred, a low rumble that permeated her being. He shifted position so that he could lick her other nipple and she moaned at the feel of his rough tongue against her nub and his long white-blond hair trailing over her skin. When he rose up again, he focused on trailing the twin cherry blossoms down the line of her belly to the star charm at her navel. He circled it, his face a mask of concentration as he teased and tantalized her.

In all her life, Awai had never experienced anything like this. How could such a large, powerful, and dominant man be so sweet and gentle?

He continued his trek, feathering her skin with soft caresses from the twin blossoms as he headed to her waxed mound. There he feathered them across the soft skin, as if to touch every bit of it without delving into her slit. Awai bit the inside of her lower lip and she grew even wetter between her legs.

"Spread your thighs as wide as possible," he ordered.

Awai raised her knees and opened herself to him. She

hoped he would relieve some of her need for him by touching her clit, but he barely skimmed the lips of her pussy before moving along the inside of one thigh. He raised himself so that he could easily trace the blossoms down her leg and lightly brushed them across the sensitive spot at the back of her knee.

Awai's thighs trembled from her intense desire for Ty and she didn't know how much longer she could take this sweet torture. When he teased the inside of her ankle, she moaned at the exquisite sensations. It was incredible, to be wearing only this man's collar and nipple rings, to be covered in cherry blossoms, and to be stroked from head to toe by the sweet smelling blossoms.

After he reached her toes and brushed the cherry blossoms across them, he moved to her other foot and began the journey back up. He worked his way from her instep to the inside of her ankle to the backside of her knee. After stroking the sensitive skin there, he moved up her leg to the juncture of her thighs, where he stopped and looked at her.

"Do you wish me to touch you here?" he murmured as he brushed the cherry blossoms over her folds so lightly that she gripped the bedcovers tight to keep from crying out.

"You know I do." Awai's gaze met his. "I need you."

Ty smiled, a completely dominant male smile that told her she belonged to him and he intended to take her, to make love to her, but in his own time. "Wait, my tigress. Soon I will thrust inside you and claim you for all eternity.

I will take you beyond this realm and we shall go there together."

He eased off the bed and she couldn't help another whimper from escaping. He moved so that he was between her thighs, his face so close to her slit that she could feel his warm breath upon her folds.

Ty inhaled deeply of his mate's scent. It soared through his being, causing his senses to take flight. He growled, barely able to restrain himself now that he was between her thighs.

With his jaws clenched, Ty brought the pair of blossoms to her folds and brushed her clit. Awai gasped and her hips arched up off the bed before settling back onto the covers. But her thighs trembled and he knew she was on the fine edge of control, just as he was.

"Do not climax without me," he commanded, and Awai whimpered again.

Her scent and her sweet cream were an aphrodisiac to his keen weretiger senses while he studied her beautiful quim illuminated by dancing candlelight. He loved her folds, the curves and the contours. He loved the way the lips of her slit grew swollen with need and her folds red from the rush of blood.

Ty released the blossoms and slid one finger into her tight core. Awai moaned and raised her back up off the bed. "I don't know if I can hold back," she said as she squirmed beneath his gaze.

He lowered his head and nuzzled the lips of her quim. "You must, my love."

Ty lapped at her then, her taste flowing over his tongue like the sweetest cherry wine. This time she cried out and he felt the beginning vibrations of her nearing the peak. Although he wished to taste more of her, he forced himself to stop, to pull away from her and to slide his finger from her core.

Awai's body was so tense from need that when Ty finally rose up between her thighs she thought she might climax at the mere sight of her man. He braced his hands to either side of her breasts and slowly lowered himself so that his cock lay hard against her mound, the cherry blossoms crushed between them. He studied her, just holding her gaze as he kept himself still. His long blond hair fell forward, brushing her nipples, the feeling as hot as a candle's flame.

"Make love to me, Ty." She clenched her thighs around his hips as if she could hold this powerful man there. "Please."

He brought one hand to his cock and positioned it at her core, never taking his gaze from hers. "Watch me, Awai," he said as he slid partway in. "Watch me make love to you and make you mine evermore."

"Yes." She arched up to him, trying to take him deeper. "I belong to you."

Ty thrust deep, burying his cock completely within her core. Awai gasped. He stretched her, filled her like no one else could. In every way, from her body to her soul to her heart.

Slowly Ty began to move in and out of her, his balls slapping against her, his thrusts deep and purposeful.

Awai held on to him, running her hands down his back to his tight ass, where she stopped and held on. She loved the feel of his muscles beneath her palms, the way his body moved against her, his scent and his sweat mingling with hers.

Closer and closer she came to climax, and when she was barely holding on by a thread she clenched her fingers into his ass. "Now, Ty! I can't hold on much longer."

"Yes, my tigress." He thrust harder. "Climax for me now!"

Awai's cry echoed throughout the room. Her orgasm made her feel as though she was spinning out of control. A burst of color filled her mind, and like the aurora it faded into shimmering waves. Somehow her consciousness recognized Ty's roar as he came. His cock pulsated in her channel, drawing out her orgasm, making it throb from her ass to her core to her belly.

Ty rolled to the side, cradling Awai close to his chest. She smelled his sweat and her own, his come and her juices. Their breathing was ragged as he tucked her head under his chin and held on to her.

"I love you, Awai," he murmured. "You are everything to me."

"I love you, Ty," she said before slipping into a deep sleep.

Awai wandered alone through the cherry trees, blossoms floating around her in the afternoon sunshine. The blossoms spiraled down toward the earth like pinwheels, and covered the ground in a soft and sweetly scented blanket beneath her bare feet. The cherry trees were in bloom throughout the spring, Ty had explained long ago. It wasn't until summer that the trees began to bear fruit—cherries as large as plums by midsummer. His subjects used them to make the finest jams, pies, cakes, and treats in all of Tarok. People would come for miles just to purchase such delights from the Kingdom of Clubs.

The day was so beautiful and filled with such anticipation. But still that sense of dread hung onto the edge of her consciousness. She didn't understand why she should feel a hint of darkness when she should be happy and excited.

A gust of wind caused Awai's robes to swirl around her legs. The silky material of her robe pressed against her nipples that were always hard thanks to the charms she constantly wore. Ty's collar felt snug around her neck and as always made her feel secure . . . and loved.

What would her nieces think? Did they wear collars, too?

According to Ty's sentinels and his keen weretiger senses, her nieces and their families would arrive soon.

So many emotions and feelings nearly overwhelmed Awai. Anticipation and excitement, yet nervousness and uncertainty warred within her. How did a person greet the ones she loved and hadn't seen for a year to three years? This was different from having a family member abroad or in the military for a great length of time. She had truly thought her nieces had been kidnapped and were in danger . . . or perhaps even dead. She'd cried over them, worried about them, grieved for them.

And when she found out they were alive, well, and happy, her joy had been immense. Yet there still remained that tiny bit of uncertainty—she only knew what Ty had told her. Even though she trusted him with all her heart, she had to see for herself, and had to hold each one of them in her arms.

"Tigress," came Ty's low rumble behind her. "It is time."

Awai turned and gave her king a tremulous smile. "I'm scared, Ty. I'm happy, but I'm scared, too."

He reached for her faster than she could catch her breath and brought her close to his chest. "There is nothing to fear, my sweet. Only joy will your heart know this day."

She hugged him, letting his strength feed her, drinking in the smell of him, the feel of him in her arms. She tilted her head back and this time her smile was confident. "I love you."

Ty hooked his finger under her chin and returned her smile. "I know."

Awai laughed and Ty kept his arm possessively around her shoulders as they walked to the front of the palace. It was an impressive entrance that they rarely used as they tended to prefer the back entrance leading to the cherry grove.

At the front entrance, green granite steps marched down to a circular driveway that looped around a marble fountain of two enormous white-and-black striped tigers in battle. Flowers in every shade of the rainbow spilled down the sides of the steps and surrounded the driveway. The air smelled fresh and clean from the recent rains mixed with the intoxicating perfume of all the flowers. Birds sang and water splashed in the fountain, echoing in that moment of near silence.

Then in the distance she heard the sound of horses' hooves—or rather *jul*, the name for the horselike beasts the people of Tarok often used for transportation. Carriages creaked and happy voices carried on the warm spring air.

Awai clenched her hands into fists, her nails biting into her palms as she bounced up and down on the balls of her bare feet. She was so nervous and so anxious that she nearly broke into a run just to reach her nieces as quickly as possible.

And then they rounded the corner. First a sleek white coach with a red heart symbol on its side, drawn by four *jul* that were the color of liquid silver. Following behind was a beautiful black coach with a gold spade on each of the doors, and the coach was drawn by four black *jul*. Lastly came a dark red coach with a gold filigree diamond symbol on its door and the *jul* that drew it were golden.

The moment the coaches came to a stop, each of the doors burst open and out tumbled a small herd of young tigers, followed by three women and three men, followed by a calico cat with a regal bearing. For what seemed like an eternity, Awai just stared at Annie, Alexi, and Alice, who looked so different, yet were the women she loved more than anything. She was vaguely aware of tears streaming down her cheeks and Ty's protective arm around her shoulders.

The next thing she knew she was swallowed up in a swirl of laughter and tears and joy unlike anything she had ever known. She cried and kissed and hugged them each so much that she was lost in a sea of emotion and couldn't see through her blur of tears.

When they finally separated long enough for Awai to catch her breath, she wiped the tears from her eyes with the sleeves of her robe and looked helplessly at her nieces. "God, I missed you all so much. I thought I'd never see you again."

Alice threw her arms around Awai again. "Three years, Awai. I can't believe it's been so very long." She pulled away and held Awai's hands. Alice's turquoise eyes were wide, tears sparkling on her lashes. "I'm so happy I could just burst."

Awai drank in the sight of Alice, who was wearing a sparkling yet practically sheer robe that barely concealed her nipples and her mound. Her white-blond hair gleamed in the sunlight and her eyes sparkled. At her throat was a wide diamond collar with hearts made of red rubies. But more than anything else, the change in Alice's bearing was what surprised Awai the most. She had an air of happiness, of confidence in herself and those around her.

"I can hardly speak," Awai said, trying to swallow the lump in her throat. "Do you have any idea how long three years is?"

"Makes you want to kick someone's ass, doesn't it?" came Alexi's voice, and Awai had to smile as she faced her take-no-prisoners niece who had been a powerful San Francisco sexual harassment lawyer. Alexi gave a teasing grin and hugged Awai. "Damn it, but I missed you." Alexi tossed her auburn hair over her shoulder and raised one eyebrow at Ty, who had stepped away from the flurry of hugging and crying women.

"Do not worry, Queen Alexi," he said with a soft chuckle. "I fear for my manhood too much to cross you."

Alexi's collar of white diamonds with black diamond spades glittered as she put her hands on her leather-clad hips and gave him a mock frown. "Just see that you remain in line, mister."

With a laugh, Awai turned to the quietest of her nieces, Annie, who was holding her calico cat, Abra. They enveloped each another in a fierce hug and Abra gave an irritated *yerowl* and slipped from between them.

Awai kept her hold on Annie and whispered, "When I came back the next day and you and Abra were gone, I couldn't forgive myself for leaving you alone that night."

Annie leaned back and brushed a tear from Awai's face. "I'm sorry this has been so hard on you, more than on any of us. But I can't tell you how happy we all are, and how wonderful it is to have you here with all of us."

Awai couldn't help but notice how radiant Annie was and how vibrant. She, too, had a collar of diamonds, but with red rubies in the shape of diamonds around it. She wore an almost sheer crimson dress that reached midthigh.

Her dark hair flowed around her shoulders and her gold-framed glasses glinted in the sunlight.

"This world is almost too perfect," Awai said, looking to each cousin and to the powerful men standing behind them.

"It's far from perfect," Annie said as she took Awai's hands in hers. "This world has much to strive for and many dangers to overcome. But it's the love that we feel for our mates, our children, and each other that makes it even more special."

At the thought of children, Awai glanced to the eleven tiger cubs pouncing on their uncles who were now sitting on the palace steps. Ty and the other kings had joined the fray and were playing with the children who frequently shifted from tiger to child and back again. They giggled, mewled, shouted, and growled, and Awai felt that lump rise in her throat again at the incredible joy of the moment.

"I can't believe you're all mothers." Awai looked to each of her nieces who beamed with pride at their children. "*Mothers.*"

Alice laughed and put her arm around Awai and squeezed her. "Just wait until you have cubs of your own."

Alexi nodded. "I didn't think I wanted to have children, but I wouldn't change a single thing about my life. I love them so much, I can't imagine life without my sons and daughter."

Awai gave a half smile but remained silent as she watched Ty laughing and playing with the cubs like a big kid himself. She remembered how much fun he had picking out gifts for his nieces and nephews and how he spoke of them with such pride. He would make such a wonderful father.

She had never planned on having children, but so much had changed. Could she give Ty what he obviously wanted—a family of his own?

CHAPTER FOURTEEN

AWAI LAUGHED AS SHE AND THE CUBS PLAYED hide-and-seek in the cherry trees. Her family had been at the palace for a week now, and she had come to love romping through the palace grounds with the children. She had even grown comfortable in her aunt's role, and felt like she could manage the little buggers all on her own.

Everyone had gone into the village but Awai had offered to stay and play with the cubs, just to prove it—to herself, more than anyone. Besides, the kingdom was well guarded, but she couldn't help feeling a sense of dread after all the dreams she'd been having. She felt like it was her duty, somehow, to stay with the children.

Ty had stayed, too, but had been called back inside the palace on urgent business with Kir and Rafe. Ty had kissed her and promised to "rescue" her from all the children as soon as possible. Awai dearly loved all eleven of her great nephews and nieces, but regularly they fought and argued and pouted and threw temper tantrums, just like other children, so it was always good to have adult reinforcements around. Especially since there were eleven of the little monsters—er, darlings.

The four youngest toddlers played in the middle of a group of cherry trees. Three of them rolled around, play-fighting as young tiger cubs, while Johanna sat off to herself, snapping Awai's whip the best she could with her little hands. Johanna had latched onto the whip from the moment she'd arrived at the castle. She'd refused to let anyone take it away from her, although she would let Awai play with her and the whip sometimes.

Blossoms and grass felt soft beneath Awai's bare feet as she quietly searched for each of the seven older children hiding in the trees. Sunlight dappled the orchard, leaves waving and rustling in a balmy breeze. Her silk robe swirled around her ankles and her hair lifted from her face as she quietly made her way over the cherry blossom carpet to where she spied a small twitching tiger tail peeking out from around a *ch'tok* tree.

Very slowly she crept up on the child and then pounced on the tail. It was Jennifer, and the cub shifted into a little girl and shrieked with laughter. "You found me Auntie Awai!"

Awai kissed the two-year-old on the cheek and sent her to play with the other little ones in the middle of the orchard. It amazed Awai how much faster these children grew in comparison to Earth children.

Gradually Awai tracked down each child until there

were only the two oldest, Lexi and Lance. The rest of the children were playing tag in the middle of the orchard. The sound of laughter, giggles, and shrieks filled the afternoon air. Johanna still sat off to the side, quietly snapping Awai's whip and swirling it around like a snake in the grass. Awai grinned at the thought of Johanna growing up to turn this male-dominated society on its ear by becoming a Domme.

Awai eased between a pair of cherry trees when she spotted a white tiger's tail. Surely that was Lexi or Lance, although she'd never realized that one had a tail so white instead of striped.

A twig snapped under Awai's bare foot just as she was reaching for the tail. Then, so fast, before she knew what was happening, the tiger whirled.

It wasn't one of the children. It was a huge pure white tiger.

The one from her dreams.

The full-grown beast pounced on Awai, slamming her flat on her back and knocking the breath from her lungs. A slash of hair from one side of the beast's face was missing, a jagged scar. Its eyes were wild and glowed a fearsome red.

Terror flooded Awai as she stared up at the menacing tiger whose teeth were bared. The fear was not so much for herself as for the children. The tiger pinned Awai by her shoulders and the big cat's rear paws kept her from moving her legs.

Awai didn't want to die, but it was more important

that the children were safe. She did the only thing she could think of.

"Run!" she screamed. "Run to the palace as fast as you can."

The tiger raised its head to look at the children, who screamed and shifted to tigers and started to bound away, only to find themselves surrounded by a pack of enormous black-and-white tigers.

"Are you weretigers?" Awai asked, her voice trembling as she looked up at the white beast with the fiercely glowing red eyes. "Please let the children go. Kill me if you have to, but let the children go. *Please.*"

So easy . . . Awai heard in her head—a feminine voice. *With the force of my mindspells it was so easy to break through the palace borders. Did my brother think he could keep me out?*

The words entered Awai's mind, just like Ty communicated with her when he was in weretiger form. The tiger raised her head and looked to the children, who had been herded into a small group.

Then she backed away, freeing Awai, but standing close enough that with a single swipe of her paw she could rip out Awai's throat.

I slipped through their nets so easily, the tiger said in Awai's mind. *I have powers none of you can comprehend. Nothing can stop me.*

"You're Mikaela." Awai swallowed and pushed herself up to a sitting position. "Your brothers thought you died when you fell from the cliff."

In the next moment the tiger shifted into a woman with wheat-blond hair, a black leather jumpsuit, and a whip clutched in her hand. Unlike the oil painting Awai had seen of Mikaela, this woman had a jagged scar running from her temple to her chin. It was dark pink against her fair skin, the only mar on an otherwise beautiful face.

The woman brought up her free hand and traced the scar. "This is what they have done to me."

"Karn tried to save you." Awai rose slowly to her feet, hoping the woman wouldn't shift back into a tiger and attack. A tiger scared the shit out of her, but a woman was something she could battle. "Annie told me he lunged for you, but you slipped and fell to the rocks below. They thought you'd been swept out to the sea."

"They were right . . . I was swept out to sea . . ." She began running the length of the whip through her hands, slowly, surely, as if testing its strength, preparing to use it. From her own extensive knowledge, Awai knew a whip like that could flay a person's flesh if used intentionally to injure.

"Please don't do this." Awai clenched her hands into fists. "Your brothers loved you so much. They still do. They want the sister back that they've always known and cared for. I've heard it from them myself."

The red in the woman's eyes seemed to fade and Awai could almost see blue as Mikaela said, "That was long ago."

Awai chanced a step forward. "It's never too late."

Mikaela's eyes flashed and glowed an even brighter red. "He—I want all of Tarok as my own."

The children whimpered and Awai tore her gaze from Mikaela's to see that they were nearly surrounded by at least ten enormous white-and-black striped weretigers. Instinctively Awai counted the cubs. Eight? Her heart leapt with terror. There should have been eleven. Lance and Lexi must still be hiding, and Johanna was missing.

"So, three of the cubs are gone." Mikaela narrowed her eyes, and at Awai's small gasp, the woman added, "I read it in your thoughts."

She raised her head and said to the nearest weretiger, "Three of the cubs are hiding in the bushes."

While Mikaela was giving the order, Awai heard a soft sound behind her, and then hard leather pressed into her hand. The moment she gripped it, Awai knew it was her leather whip. Johanna had brought it to her.

Awai reached for the memory of her subspace experiences, the many times she had diverted her mind to delay orgasm, and let her mind go as blank as possible to keep Mikaela from reading her thoughts and finding out that Johanna had brought the whip. Awai gripped the handle tight behind her, hoping that Mikaela and the other weretigers hadn't noticed. "Please let the children go."

Mikaela turned her red gaze back to Awai. "Don't you understand? This is what we've been waiting for. A chance to end the Tarok way of life. To cut my brothers to the quick by destroying all that they hold dear. If we tear out their hearts, tearing off their heads won't be far behind."

Awai heard the words, but something wasn't registering. Why was Mikaela talking? Why didn't she simply attack? It was as though she was holding something back—struggling against a part of herself. And there was something more. Awai felt a distinctly male presence, yet Mikaela was clearly a woman, and she was Ty's sister.

Her dreams of late merged with the moment, making everything seem so surreal. A white tiger cloaked in black. A white tiger at the end of a tunnel. A white tiger in a cage . . .

The woman straightened, her red gaze focusing on Awai. "You are different from the other females," Mikaela said. "Stronger. Perhaps you will be kept and taken to Malachad once everyone else has been destroyed."

Awai clenched the handle of her whip tighter. "Why?"

"Because it pleases—" She faltered as if struggling to form her thoughts. "It pleases me."

Mikaela turned toward the tigers guarding the children. Awai was tempted to use her whip to rip Mikaela's own whip from her hand. But what if the tigers attacked the children?

The woman's voice grew deep, almost like a man's. "Prepare to rid Tarok of its heirs."

The tigers shifted into men and women, clothed in black and each bearing daggers that gleamed ominously in the sunshine.

The children huddled in the center of the orchard, their small faces full of fear.

A tiger stepped from the orchard and shifted to a man. "The scent of two cubs leads toward the palace. I fear they have gone to warn the king. We best be done with these and come back for the rest."

"Yes . . ." Mikaela gave a slow nod. "We will slay my

brothers and their mates while they are grieving for their children."

"Wait!" A woman's shout echoed through the orchard. Mikaela raised her whip as Kalina burst into the small clearing, her hands held high, her dark hair streaming down her back, her black robes molded against her slender body.

"You wish to die with the children, sorceress?" Mikaela said with one eyebrow raised.

"The cards have finally revealed the truth." It was obvious Kalina was slightly out of breath from running from the palace.

Mikaela smirked, her eyes glowing a more ominous red. "Truth? The truth is that you will soon be dead."

"No." Kalina lowered her hands and slowly walked toward the woman. "You are not yourself. For well over two decades you have been under the control of the King of Malachad, the true sorcerer behind all this hate and destruction of the Tarok way of life. He wants to rule over Tarok and Malachad and to do that he has used you."

Again that flash of uncertainty in Mikaela's eyes, then again replaced by a red haze. "I seek revenge on my brothers and my parents. That is the truth."

As Kalina and Mikaela spoke to one another, Awai slowly eased toward the cubs and the men and women standing ready to slice the children's throats. Awai was careful to keep the whip behind her back.

"You fight against this possession." Kalina radiated an aura of power, her fire-ice eyes brilliant as she came within feet of Mikaela. "These *bakir* do not serve you. They serve the King of Malachad. If you told them to stand down they would not, because they would not disobey Balin, the true sorcerer."

"I control Balin." Mikaela shook her head, the scar across her cheek whitening as her features tensed. "The *bakirs* serve me and *my* will."

"Your will is not your own," Kalina said softly and extended her hand. "Touch me and you will see all that I have seen. The cards decreed it."

With a scowl and a jerk, as if fighting herself, or fighting another force, Mikaela snatched Kalina by the wrist and dragged the sorceress closer.

Mikaela's jaw went slack, her knees giving way slightly, as if she could barely hold herself up. Her body trembled and her expression became one of anguish and pain. Her eyes flashed from red to blue and back to red again.

The sorceress's expressions mirrored Mikaela's and her eyes filled with tears, but she did not break away.

The *bakirs* stirred and looked at one another, their daggers still at the ready. Clearly they were confused and didn't understand what was happening.

Mikaela's entire body shook and her face was contorted by expressions that flashed through her one by one—of pain, fear, hatred, joy, then back to terror and anger again.

"You are powerful, Mikaela," Kalina said, her voice low but trembling. "You are so powerful that Balin needs you to do his bidding so that he can control Tarok. You have the strength to force him from your mind. Only you."

Mikaela released Kalina's wrist and clenched her fists.

Her face contorted as she struggled to take command of her soul. Her body trembled and sweat rolled down her face.

The *bakirs* looked even more disturbed. Their uncertainty made it obvious they had never seen their queen act in such a manner.

The red haze to Mikaela's eyes flared then faded, leaving only clear, clear blue. "Who am I?" she whispered. "A beast. A foul beast."

"You have not been of your own mind for countless years," Kalina said softly, so that only Mikaela could hear. "This will be difficult. Long has the King of Malachad controlled you—since you were but a teenager, before you were wed to him. The fight is not over for your soul."

"Shall we kill them now?" One *bakir* said, grabbing Paula by the scruff of her neck and bringing his dagger perilously close to the toddler's throat.

"You must pretend, Mikaela," Kalina urged in a whisper Awai barely heard. "Do not let them know what you have seen."

Awai had managed to get within five feet of the *bakir* threatening Paula. She was ready—at the right moment, she would do whatever she had to do. She would give her life for these children.

Please, please, let Mikaela believe the sorceress . . .

Mikaela straightened and clenched her whip. "I will kill the first cub myself," she said with an air of command. Fear leapt again inside Awai, but Mikaela's eyes were still a clear blue.

She turned to Kalina, her gaze holding a message. "You will die with the rest, sorceress. Join Ty's woman."

With purpose to her steps, Mikaela strode up to the children and her *bakirs.* She placed her hands on her hips and gave a ruthless smile. "Long have I waited for this day."

Awai's heart dropped. She couldn't see Mikaela's eyes. Was she back under the king's control?

With a snap of her whip, Mikaela caught the *bakir* threatening Paula by the throat and wrenched it so hard the sound of his neck breaking shattered the quiet in the orchard.

Everything next happened in a blur.

Children screamed and ran while Kalina herded them to safety.

The crack of Awai's whip rang out as she used it to tear a dagger from the hand of one *bakir.*

Mikaela transformed into a tiger and attacked her own *bakirs.* She ripped the throat of one man before he could shift.

With quick snaps of her whip, Awai managed to disarm three of the *bakirs.* In the next moment they shifted into tigers and bore down on her and she screamed in terror.

Tremendous roars came from behind Awai and she knew she was going to die. But then at least a dozen tigers and two wolves bounded past her, barreling into the tigers that had been about to attack Awai and into those fighting Mikaela.

Everything happened so fast that Awai didn't have time to breathe. She cracked her whip as a tiger headed her way, but another tiger rose up on his hind legs. Awai saw the club shape in the fur on his belly and her heart raced with fear as she recognized Ty. He battled the *bakir*, flinging the beast to the ground and breaking its neck with his massive jaws.

Roars and screams filled the orchard as tigers battled, and the grassy clearing became covered in bodies and blood.

"Do not hurt Mikaela!" Kalina shouted but her words were lost in the tremendous noise filling the clearing.

Tigers lay dead around them while others bounded into the cherry grove and were followed by Ty's guards.

And then everything went silent, save for the wind rustling through the cherry trees.

The largest tiger with the pattern of a heart on his powerful front leg had one tiger pinned to the ground. The last living *bakir* in the clearing—the white tiger.

She was on her back, her throat exposed for Jarronn to rip out by clamping his tremendous jaws around her jugular.

Slay me now, came Mikaela's voice, filling Awai's mind and obviously those around her. *I deserve to die.*

Yes, you will die. Jarronn's voice rang ominously in their thoughts. *You attempted to kill our children. You have tried to kill our mates.*

"You must listen to me and what the cards have said." Kalina ran forward and touched Jarronn on his back. "Mikaela fought to save the cubs, my king."

The High King turned his feline gaze on her and narrowed his blue tiger eyes. *She has terrorized our people for decades, has prevented our race from growing and forcing us to near extinction.*

Beneath his tremendous paws, Mikaela shifted into a woman. Her expression held no fear, only sorrow. Her scar was a bright slash against her pale features, and her eyes glittered as if she held back tears.

She tipped back her head, fully exposing her throat. "You are right," she said. "Please do not show me mercy. I could not bear it."

Ty's emotions ranged from anger to uncertainty to sadness for the sister he had known and loved. He joined Kalina and said, "Let us hear what Kalina has to say. What the cards have told her."

The High King backed away and shifted into a man. He rose to a standing position and his face was stern as he looked at his sister.

He turned his dark expression to Kalina. "Speak."

The sorceress kept her head high and her gaze level with Jarronn's. "The cards have always told me there was a threat to the south and that Mikaela kept our people from conceiving." Jarronn scowled, and Kalina hurried to continue, "But what they didn't tell me until recently was that Mikaela has been under King Malachad's control all these many years. Even before she wed him he used his own power and the power of his *bakirs* to influence her. She is by far the most talented of all the royalty in Tarok as well as in the Kingdom of Malachad. Balin recognized that and used her."

"This is true?" The High King said, his expression unreadable. "The cards have made this clear?"

"Yes, Milord." Kalina bowed her head. "I am sorry I could not interpret this until now. Until it was almost too late."

"It does not matter," came Mikaela's soft voice as she pushed herself up so that she was on her knees. "My crimes are unforgivable. And I do not know that I can keep him out of my mind, keep him from controlling me again. What if I hurt one of you or your people, or one of the children?" Tears were rolling down her cheeks and her voice trembled. "You must kill me now to ensure you are all safe."

King Jarronn hesitated, his face reflecting a mixture of rage and horror. After a long, tense moment, he held out his hand to Mikaela. She hesitated, then allowed him to pull her to a standing position. She stood before him, her head held high and a world of pain in her eyes.

"I can feel him trying to force himself back into my head, Jarronn." A tear rolled down her cheek. "I don't know if I'm strong enough to fight him off much longer."

Jarronn reached out and brought his sister roughly into his arms and pressed her head to his shoulder as he hugged her. "We will help you. We are family."

"I do not know that I can be saved." Mikaela gently pushed at his chest so that they were slightly parted. "It has been far too long."

Karn shoved his way in between the two, and Jarronn backed away. Karn's expression was one of sadness as he traced his finger along Mikaela's scar, a soft touch that made her visibly shudder. "On that dark stormy night, before you fell, I told you that we love you and that we know there is good in you. Together we can keep you safe. We can be family again."

"I love you all." Another tear eased over Mikaela's cheek. "But do you not understand? I am dangerous."

This time it was Darronn who came to stand before Mikaela. "I have ached for you. Have felt betrayed because I thought you and I were so close. But then you turned on us. Or so I thought you did." Darronn took her hands in his. "I cannot tell you the joy this brings me. To know that my sister was not of herself and that she is still here for us to love."

"It is too late for my soul," she whispered.

Ty made his way to his sister and Darronn stepped away. Ty's heart sang as he looked down at his little sister. "You are ours again." He crushed her against his chest. "We are family again."

"I love you all," she said as she pushed away from Ty. Tears rolled freely now and her expression was one of anguish. "That is why I must leave."

And with that she turned, shifting into a tiger. She bounded into the cherry trees and vanished into the grove. For a moment everyone stared with stunned expressions at where she had disappeared.

The men started after her, but Kalina shouted, "Wait!" She turned to the four kings and gave a reverent bow. "Long I have served you, and with the joining of Ty and Awai I will be freed of my services."

Ty felt deep sorrow at Kalina's words, and he was sure

his brothers felt the same. She had been friend, lover, and advisor to them all. "You will always have a home with us," Ty said.

"Nevertheless, it is time to find my own way, my own life." She raised her head, nodding to each of the kings. "It has been my pleasure."

In the next instant Kalina shifted into a tiger, turning away from everyone gathered around her. She paused and looked over her shoulder. *I will follow Mikaela and together we will make our way. One day we shall meet again.*

And with that she bounded through the cherry trees and out of their lives.

The two wolves who had helped slay the *bakirs* shifted into Lord Kir and Rafe.

Rafe approached the High King. "I will see that they both remain safe." He gave a slight bow and transformed into a wolf. At a casual lope he scented the trail and followed the weretigresses.

CHAPTER FIFTEEN

AWAI SAT BESIDE THE POND BEHIND THE PALace, her legs drawn up and her chin resting on her knees. So much had happened in the last several weeks of her life that she could barely fathom all the changes.

She had been taken from the world she knew and fallen in love with the mysterious realm of Tarok. More than that, she had fallen in love with a dominant, beautiful weretiger. She had learned to submit, learned the truth of her own strength and power. She had even helped fight a sorcerer and his minions to defend the lives of her now large and growing family.

And now, it was time to lay it all on the line, to decide now and forever where she would live, who she would be—and who she would be with.

Ty had scheduled the joining ceremony for a week after the *bakirs* attack, and the day had finally arrived.

Today, if she decided it was the right thing to do, Awai would wed Ty.

She rocked slightly as she watched the vividly colored fish in the pool. Thoughts of the last time she had sat here came to her mind and she smiled at the memory. She and Ty had ended up going to the village to buy gifts for every member of their family.

Her smile faded as she reached down and plucked a white starflower from beside her. She twirled the bloom between her thumb and forefinger, her mind lost in the past, the present, and the future.

She held the bloom in her palm and the breeze caught it up and lazily brought it to the surface of the pond where it twirled and eased across the clear surface.

As much as she loved her nieces and nephews, and as much as she loved Ty, it was still hard for her to imagine having children. Ty deserved to be a father—he would be such a good one. But she couldn't begin to picture herself as a mother, and didn't know if she really wanted to. Ty had explained how she could only conceive if he released his seed when they both reached simultaneous climax, and that was only if she was in heat. He had said it would be her choice when the time came.

Awai braced her hands to either side of her, closed her eyes, and tilted her face to the sky. Sunshine warmed her face, caressing her with gentle rays of hope and love.

A mere fraction of a moment before his lips met hers, Awai sensed Ty's presence. His lips were firm yet gentle, his taste and smell seeping into her blood, into her being.

How could she refuse him anything?

How could she leave him?

Ty drew back and Awai opened her eyes to see his serious expression. "What is wrong, my tigress? For days I have seen something haunting your eyes. I thought perhaps it was what happened when the *bakirs* attacked, but I sense it is more."

"Hold me," Awai whispered, needing the comfort of his embrace. Ty wrapped his powerful arm around her shoulders and drew her to his bare chest. He smelled of sun and wind, and his own elemental scent.

"What is it, love?" he asked as he stroked dark hair from her eyes.

She swallowed and took a deep breath. "I don't think I can marry you, join with you."

For a single moment Ty's heart ceased to beat. "What are you saying, Awai?"

"It really scared me when the children were in danger." She pulled away from him to meet his gaze and he saw her eyes glistening with tears. "The life of a child is so fragile, and I don't know if I can be a mother. I know it's important to you—you make a wonderful uncle and I know you'd be the perfect father. But as for me . . . I'm not sure I can do it."

Ty gave her a gentle smile. He enjoyed his nephews and nieces, and if he and Awai did not have children of their own he would always have his brothers' children to love and shower with affection. What was more important to him was Awai's love and her happiness.

"The choice will be yours." He squeezed her tight to him.

She gave a shuddering sigh and shook her head. "You are so wonderful with the kids. You deserve children of your own."

"I do not need children to feel complete." He caught her chin in his large palm and brushed a tear from her cheek with his thumb. "You complete me, Awai."

Awai searched Ty's eyes. They held nothing but the truth of his heart and his love for her. He had never lied to her, had never held anything back from her. Always he had been truthful and had done what he thought was right.

Her face went serious and she asked, "What about an heir for your kingdom?"

"Lance will likely inherit the Kingdom of Hearts," he said with a thoughtful look. "As second oldest, I think that Lexi should inherit the Kingdom of Clubs if we do not produce an heir."

Awai gave an impish grin. "What about Johanna? She's destined to be a leader among men and women. Just look at the way she wields that whip."

Ty laughed and shook his head. "Perhaps, tigress. Perhaps."

"You are a wonderful man." Awai hugged him tight. "What did I ever do to deserve you?"

"I am the one who is thankful to the stars for you, tigress," he murmured as he kissed her hair. "I am the one who is blessed."

* * *

Puffy blue-green clouds floated across the endless aqua sky on the evening of their joining day. Awai stood at the window of their bedchamber, staring out at the sky as her nieces fussed over preparations and laughed and chattered behind her.

A feeling of contentment settled over Awai. She had met a man beyond her wildest dreams, a man who loved her and was willing to listen to her heart and to allow her the freedom she needed. A man who dominated her, but who would never harm her in any way.

"Come now," Alice said, and Awai turned from the window. Alice tossed her white-blond hair over her shoulder. "It's time you put on your wedding dress."

Awai smiled and let her black robe fall into a swirl of silk at her feet. She was naked, but in the two weeks since her nieces had been here, she had learned that none of them batted an eye at anyone being around them in the buff.

She was surprised, however, when Alexi plucked the nipple charms off her nipples. "Since Kalina isn't here, I guess this is up to me," Alexi said, her aqua eyes focused on her task. Awai frowned but didn't argue as her black collar was also removed from her throat.

Annie pushed her gold-rimmed glasses up the bridge of her nose then helped Awai into the white silk robe that barely concealed her lush figure. The robe was fitted and had an off-the-shoulder cut to it that dipped down to fasten just beneath her belly button, exposing the star charm at her navel. The creamy silk barely covered the sides of her breasts and her nipples.

The robe was fastened from below Awai's navel and down to her mons, but then flared out, exposing her thighs and her long legs. It was also cut low in the back, all the way down to the base of her spine. The sleeves were long and covered more than the rest of the robe did.

Awai felt something roll over her feet and laughed when she saw Abra playing with her black collar, batting it around and flipping it into the air. "All right, you little imp," she murmured as she bent to scratch the calico cat behind her ears. The cat had her own red collar with white diamonds glistening along the band. Awai straightened and put her hands on her hips. "Just be sure to keep your paws to yourself when it comes to my wedding robe."

Alice laughed and sprinkled cherry blossoms in Awai's hair while Annie handed her a bouquet made of cherry blossoms.

"Perfect," Alice announced. "You make the most beautiful bride."

Awai smiled, but her insides felt like she was going to explode with nervousness. "Will the children be at the ceremony?"

"Are you kidding?" Alexi rolled her eyes. "Eleven children racing around? I don't *think* so."

"The nannies are taking care of them," Annie said. "They need to make sure the children get to bed at a decent time."

"Not to mention they are being heavily guarded." Alexi's hands were on her hips. "We are not about to take any chances with our children. The way those *bakirs* slipped through the guards—it was like they used magic or something."

"Mikaela is no longer under the King of Malachad's control," Annie said with a hopeful note to her voice. "If only she can continue to fight him off, she will remain free."

Awai nodded. "I hope for her sake and ours that she wins in the war for her soul."

When they were all ready, Awai told her nieces to go along without her. She needed a moment to herself, and then she would follow to where the ceremony would be held.

Alexi gave a small frown. "You're not going to run off on us now, and stand up the groom?"

Awai couldn't help a teasing grin. "Can't say it hasn't crossed my mind." But then her expression grew serious. "I just need a little quiet to collect my thoughts."

"All right, sugar." Annie gave Awai a quick kiss on her cheek. "You take all the time you need."

When everyone had left the bedchamber, Awai clutched her bouquet in one hand as she went to the window to stare out at the beautiful world she now lived in. No San Francisco skyline, no Chinese food from her favorite dim sum restaurant, no trolley, no corporate ladders to climb. Instead she would live in an almost medieval world run by magic and men and women, in a male-dominated society. Yet the women *were* treated as equals here, for the most part, just not when it came to sex.

Of course the women all seemed to love it, and Awai couldn't argue.

Awai sighed and touched her fingertips to the pane of glass. The aqua clouds grew into a deeper blue as they floated in the sky. It was growing darker and would soon be sunset.

She would miss so much of her former home. Sourdough bread and clam chowder, lobster and crab, the hustle and bustle of the city she loved. The broad mixture of races and cultures.

Could she do this? Could she stay in a foreign world?

All of her family was here. Her nieces—and good lord, all of their children that she had grown to love as much as Annie, Alexi, and Alice.

And Ty. She loved him more than anything.

His warm presence suddenly surrounded her. She saw his reflection in the glass the second before his arms wrapped around her waist and his chin rested on the top of her head. "You miss your world," he said simply.

Awai closed her eyes for a moment before opening them again. "It scares me to think of never again experiencing life the way I've known it for so long."

Gently taking her by the shoulders he turned her around in his embrace and she tilted her head to look up at him. "If you wish to live in your world," he said, "I would go with you."

"You would—" A prickling sensation at the back of Awai's eyes started and she bit her lip to keep from crying. "You would," she finally started again, "leave all that you know and love for me?"

He brushed away the errant tear that slipped down her cheek. "I would do whatever would make you happy. As long as we are together, that is all that matters to me."

Awai became lost in his blue gaze as she stared up at him. "But your people, your family . . ."

Ty caught her hands, crushing the bouquet of cherry blossoms between them. "I would miss them, yes. However, they would go on without me. They would continue to survive and thrive. But I could no more live without you than my world could live without the sun." He brought his forehead to hers. "I need you, Awai. You are my other half, my heart, my soul. I will do whatever will make you happy."

"You big oaf." Awai threw her arms around him, forgetting she was holding the bouquet and sending it flying across the room. "I love you so much."

He smiled as they parted, yet his eyes held seriousness. "What is it you desire?"

"I want to stay here with you." She smiled and wiped away a tear with the back of her hand. "But I would like to visit San Francisco now and again. Can we do that?"

"If it is within my power, I will do whatever I can to grant this wish." Ty held her chin and gave her a soft kiss. "Now come before everyone has the ceremony without us."

Awai laughed and Ty helped her gather the bouquet of cherry blossoms. Arm in arm, they walked through the palace to the coach waiting outside. The coach was golden with a black club upon its door. It was late evening and growing darker even as the coach pulled away from the palace.

"Where is the ceremony to take place?" she asked as she looked out the coach window.

Ty drew her close, keeping her from leaning out. "You will see."

In a matter of moments, the coach pulled up to the wharf. Awai gasped in amazement at the sight of the beautiful black yacht that was at least ten times the size of the sailboat they had made love on all those days ago. It had a golden club emblem on the side, and upon the bow *Tigress* was written in gold.

"Oh, now you're really going to make me cry," she said with a sniff. "It's beautiful, Ty."

He took her by the arm and led her down the beautiful mahogany landing and then led her up the mahogany gangplank to the yacht's main deck. Waiting there were all of her nieces and their spouses. Alexi was beaming, Alice was crying, and Annie had Abra gripped tight to her chest.

Awai's heart swelled in her throat as her future mate brought her to the head of the small crowd. The crew drew up the gangplank and the anchor, and the yacht began its trek across the dark water.

Before them the aurora borealis began to fan the sky in shimmering waves. Like starlight and rainbows blending and spilling into the water surrounding the yacht. The surface of the lake glittered and sparkled, reflecting the brilliance of the aurora. The only sounds were of the yacht making small splashing sounds as it cut through the water and night birds singing their evening song.

A balmy breeze ruffled the hem of Awai's robe and

caressed her nearly bare breasts. Ty's hair lifted from his shoulders and the club tattoo on his abs flexed as he turned her to face him.

Awai lost all sense of time or place as she looked into the eyes of her man. The bouquet slipped from her fingers, blooms spilling across the deck and scattering in the gentle wind.

"On this day I wish to join with my true mate." Ty's voice boomed in the evening silence as he brushed his fingers lightly across Awai's cheek. "I join with the woman who fills my soul with her strength, my very being with her laughter and intelligence. And the woman who fills my heart with love. Will you take me as your mate, my dear Awai?"

"Yes," she replied clearly, her voice ringing out through the night. "You are everything to me, Ty. I love you with all my heart and soul."

And she knew she was telling the truth, that she was finally and truly healed from the wounds of her past, and her heart and soul were fully hers to give once more.

Ty held out his palm and upon it appeared a glittering collar of diamonds with ebony clubs in the midst of the diamonds. "Will you wear my collar?"

Awai's voice trembled a little at the importance of the moment. "Yes." She reached up and held her dark hair away from her neck. "I belong to you."

A very male smile crossed Ty's lips as he slid his collar around her throat and fastened it. When he backed away, Awai let her hair slide over her shoulders again. She couldn't take her eyes off her beautiful man.

He held out his hand again, and in it were two diamond and ebony nipple rings. "Will you wear my insignia, showing all that you belong to me?"

Awai's heart beat faster. She loved how it had felt to wear the club charms before, and these were gorgeous and, most importantly, significant to Ty.

"Yes, I will," she said.

Ty brought up his hand and pushed aside the silk covering her left breast. Awai gasped and her nipple tightened at once. She was vaguely aware of her family and his brothers watching, but it didn't embarrass her.

He slid the loop over her nipple and tightened it with the diamond bead so that it ached and caused her pussy to drip with moisture. His eyes still focused on his task, he pushed aside the silk covering her right breast. The air had cooled and her nipple grew even harder. Ty slipped the second ring over her nipple and tightened the loop.

When he was finished, Ty cupped the back of Awai's head and brought her roughly to him. Her taut nipples and charms brushed against his heavily muscled chest and his erection pressed through his leather breeches against her almost bare belly.

"I claim you as mine," he said before crushing his mouth to hers.

The sound of cheering broke out, but Awai was lost in the kiss, lost in knowing she had joined with her soul mate. A man she could never have dreamed of finding had found her.

His mouth moved over hers, his tongue delving into

her mouth, his taste, his masculine scent seeping into her senses.

When he pulled away, he grasped her chin and smiled. “I love you, Awai.”

She caught her breath at the beauty of the moment, at the beauty of her man. “Any time, any place, any world. I love you, Ty.”

CHAPTER SIXTEEN

Awai gasped as Ty swept her up in his embrace and strode away from the bow of the yacht. She flung her arms around his neck, and her gaze was only for him as they passed their family. Awai could hear her nieces sighing and sniffling and the proud rumbles of their spouses.

Ty carried her down an ebony staircase into the depths of the yacht, down a hall lit by glowing golden orbs. He brought her into an enormous stateroom and the moment they were through the doors he used his magic to shut them behind him.

The room was filled with vases and baskets brimming with cherry blossoms. Candles in shades of pink perched upon every surface not covered by blooms, and warm yellow candlelight flickered throughout the room. The bed was enormous and the soft coverlet was covered with the sweetly scented blossoms.

Huge windows faced the northern sky and through them Awai saw the fabulous aurora, its hues of pinks and purples and golds shifting and changing into reds and blues and silvers.

Ty carefully set her down on her feet in front of the windows so that she was looking out at the aurora and her back was to him. "I can hardly believe you are mine," he murmured as he pushed away her dark hair and kissed her soft shoulder.

She shivered and tilted her head back, baring her throat to him. It felt sensual and so erotic to be standing before the aurora with her breasts naked despite her clothing, and her new nipple rings so tight that her breasts ached.

Awai sighed. "You are more than I could have hoped for." Her dark hair slid across his chest as he brought her tight against him. He brought his hands up to cup her breasts and squeezed each of her nipples.

A sigh escaped her lips as she let herself feel and experience his calloused hands upon her soft skin, his rigid erection pressing through the silk of her robes against her back. She reached up high and slid her fingers into his long blond hair as he kissed her nape. His hands worked lower, moving from her breasts to the star charm at her belly. He passed the fastening at her waist and pulled apart the front of the robe so that he could reach her bare mons.

She gasped as he slid his finger into her slit and her pussy grew even wetter. Slowly he stroked her clit, then slid his wet fingers back up over her mons, to the bare skin above her waist.

"Taste yourself," he murmured, bringing his fingers to her mouth.

Awai parted her lips and tasted the cream from between her thighs as she lightly sucked his fingers. When he slipped them from her lips she tilted her head up and back so that she could see his eyes reflecting the flickering candlelight.

Ty brought his mouth to Awai's and slipped his tongue into her depths, tasting her lips, her cream, her woman's flavor. Joy seared his veins and burned at his soul that this woman belonged to him, and him alone.

He withdrew from the kiss and for a moment gazed into her beautiful eyes. Her lips were parted, swollen, and wet from his kiss. "You are so lovely," he murmured as he reached around her and found the fastenings at her waist. He took his time, and in a slow, easy movement he released the bonds so that her robe fell open, completely exposing her to his gaze.

In the cabin window he studied her reflection, the creaminess of her skin, the glitter of the nipple charms dangling from her breasts, the light catching the star charm at her navel. Her dark hair flowed around her shoulders in contrast to her fair skin and her quim glistened with moisture.

Ty repressed a roar and the desire to thrust into his mate *now*. Instead he purred, a low rumble that rose up within his throat and reverberated throughout his being.

"My woman," he murmured as he pushed the robe slowly from her shoulders and arms. He paused partway down so that her hands were bound behind her back and her breasts thrust forward.

He lowered his mouth to her ear and felt her shiver when he whispered, "Do you enjoy being at my mercy, tigress?"

"Yes." Awai flicked her tongue against her lower lip. "I love it when you take control of me."

Ty brought his hand to her throat and caressed the diamond and ebony collar. It glittered in the window's reflection, the candlelight causing it to sparkle like sunlight on water. "You look so beautiful with my sign of ownership. Do you enjoy being owned by me?"

"More than anything." Her throat moved as she swallowed. "I am yours in every way."

His smile was so sensual that Awai's knees nearly buckled. He pushed her robe the rest of the way down her arms and let it drop in a swirl of silk around her feet. Taking her by the shoulders, Ty turned her to face him. She tilted her head up to look into his eyes and saw the love and caring he felt for her. This was not about him owning her, it was about them owning each other, and she knew he felt the same way. But he also knew how much it turned her on when he controlled her, when he dominated her.

It no longer amazed her that she was willing to give up all control to Ty. He was the only man she could ever have given herself to completely.

She reached up and touched the gold earring glinting

at his ear and slid her fingers over his stubble-roughened cheek to his lips. His hair fell long and loose about his massive shoulders and his muscles rippled as he brought his hands below her rib cage to span her small waist. She braced her hands on his shoulders to steady herself as he explored her body with his gaze and his hands.

In the next moment he cupped her naked buttocks roughly and pressed himself against her. She felt his need, felt the fine rein of control that kept him from releasing the beast that wanted to ravage her. A part of her wanted him to lose control, to take her hard and fast, but another part wanted this slow seduction.

"Let me undress you," she whispered as she brought her hands between them and to the belt around his breeches.

He rumbled, his expression fierce and filled with desire as she slowly unbuckled the club at his belt and unfastened his leather breeches. But instead of pulling out his cock, she knelt on the floor before him and unlaced one of his knee-high boots. After she unlaced the second boot he kicked them away, but she remained on her knees. She grasped his breeches and eased them down over his hips. His cock sprang free, swollen with need and lust for her.

"Hurry, woman," he growled, but she heard the love in his voice.

She didn't hurry. Instead she took her time, running her tongue along the insides of his thighs and lightly biting the skin on his knees as she pushed his breeches down to his feet. She didn't have time to tease him any further because he stepped out of his breeches and caught a handful of her hair and tilted her head back to look at him.

His eyes glowed with sensual fire. "Do you wish punishment, sweet wench?"

Awai smiled and wrapped her small hand around his large cock. "Please," she murmured before slipping her lips over the head of his erection.

Ty gave another growl and clenched his hand tighter in her hair. Awai loved the way it felt when he controlled her movements, the feel of his skin over his rigid length, the taste of his come that leaked into her mouth as she sucked his cock. She loved the wiry blond curls at the base of his shaft, loved the smell of him, the way his very presence surrounded her.

Just as she felt him stiffen, he shouted, "Enough!" and dragged her up against his muscled body and kissed her long and hard.

"I must taste you," he said in a deep rumble.

Ty's back was to the window, and as he kissed his way down her body she saw the brilliant aurora filling the night sky. His tongue flicked across one nipple to the valley of her breasts and to the other nipple as she watched the fall of glittering light outside the yacht's window.

He worked lower, flicking his tongue against her shooting-star charm before nipping at her mound. The small erotic bite caused her to gasp as more moisture flowed down her leg. Through heavy-lidded eyes she continued to watch the aurora's light show and marveled at how it danced in tune with the sensations flowing throughout her body.

In moments he reached her slit and ordered, "Widen your thighs." She obeyed and he grasped her thighs within his large grasp. He sucked her clit so hard her knees gave out and she had to grasp his shoulders to remain standing.

Ty made a deep purring sound while he licked her folds. He thrust three fingers inside her core as he continued to drive in and out of her while licking her clit.

"If you don't stop, I'm going to come," she said in a choked whisper.

"Do not climax," he ordered as he looked up at her and continued thrusting his fingers in and out of her. Teasing lights glittered in his blue eyes and she did everything she could to hold back.

With a soft laugh, Ty slipped his fingers from inside her and stood. He swept her up in his arms and carried her to the enormous bed.

He laid her gently on the bed and stared down at her. Cherry blossoms felt soft beneath her, touching her shoulders, her back, her rounded bottom, and releasing their sweet perfume.

"You make my life complete, tigress," he murmured as he ran his finger down the bridge of her nose to the tip.

She held her arms out to him. "Come to me, my king."

Ty smiled, that incredibly sexual smile that made her stomach curl and her pussy ache. With the grace of a tiger, he eased onto the bed beside her and brought her so that they were face-to-face.

Awai reached out and traced the club on his solid abs. "You are amazing," she said. "I can't believe this is all happening. That I have someone as special and perfect as you."

"I am far from perfect," he said gently, catching her hand with his. "But I do know that the most important, the most wondrous thing I have ever done in my life was to find you."

He gently pushed her on her back and she widened her legs for her mate. Ty eased between her thighs and brought his cock to her core. In a quick thrust he buried his full hard length inside her.

Awai gasped, her eyes wide as she looked up at Ty. She couldn't get over how well they fit together.

Ty took her hands and linked them with his. She kept her gaze focused on his as he slowly moved in and out of her in an easy rhythm. Candlelight illuminated his features, the fine cut of his mouth and the strong line of his jaw. His hair slipped over his shoulders and brushed against her chest with every thrust he made inside her channel.

They kept their eyes locked and their hands linked as they drove one another higher and higher toward completion. Awai felt colors and light swirl within her, like the aurora outside the stateroom window. Her abdomen clenched and her heart pounded. She didn't want to come until Ty did, and it took all her strength to hold back her climax.

Ty gritted his teeth, his look fierce yet loving all at once. She sensed his body tightening as he drew near his own climax.

"Come with me, tigress!" he ordered.

Awai cried out as her orgasm burst within her. Shades of crimson and gold filled her vision, blending to pink, to orange, to green, then to blue and silver. A rainbow of sensation filled her body, her mind, her soul.

Ty roared, a mighty bellow that seemed to shake the very structure around them. A roar that could certainly be heard from one end of the yacht to the other, from the lake to the village.

While his cock was still pulsating within her core, he rolled over on his side. Awai's head was still spinning, but the world gradually came into focus when her eyes settled on Ty's handsome face. Sweat beaded his forehead, dripped down the side of his face. His chest rose and fell, his sweaty body rubbing against hers with every breath he took. The smell of his come and the scent of her juices mingled with the sweet perfume of cherry blossoms.

Awai placed her hand on his chest, felt his heart beating beneath her fingers. "I can't wait to spend every one of my days with you, Ty. I love you so much."

Ty stroked her hair out of her eyes and smiled. "I feel the same, tigress. You are my woman, my mate, my very life. My darling Queen of Clubs."

EPILOGUE

JOHN STEELE'S HEAD SWAM FROM THE SIX VODKA martinis he'd drank and his vision blurred. He stumbled over the threshold of his Los Angeles penthouse and glared at his wide-eyed bride of two months. The little slut was only nineteen and had been a good little fuck for a while, but he was sick and tired of her. He'd started slapping her around a couple of weeks ago, but she was due for a good beating to keep her in line.

"John?" Monique had a pensive look on her face as she moved across the living room toward him. She still had a bruise on the side of her face where he'd slapped her two days ago. "What's wrong?"

The blue-eyed brunette looked too much like that whore Awai who had left him, and he'd had enough of Monique's whining. It was time he taught her a real lesson.

When she was close enough, he grabbed her by the collar of her silk blouse and dragged her toward him. "You little bitch."

Genuine fear flashed across her features and she tried to tear herself away. "Stop it!"

John laughed and she yanked back hard enough that her blouse tore. She screamed as she tripped over a footstool, landing on her back. Her blouse gaped open, and he clutched a shred of the fabric in his fist.

"Whore!" He bent and grabbed one of her wrists, and yanked her to her feet. She screamed again as he raised his fist, ready to slam it into her jaw.

Blinding white light seared his vision.

"What the fuck?" John turned toward the door. His fist was still raised and Monique still screamed and struggled to get away from him.

Something long and black lashed out at him. It wrapped around his raised fist and jerked him hard, down onto the floor so that he was on his hands and knees.

Monique had escaped John's grasp just before he hit the floor. A black snakelike whip unwound from his wrist. He scrambled to his feet, terror causing blood to roar in his ears.

The whip cracked again. This time it wrapped around his legs and yanked his feet out from under him.

His back slammed against the floor and pain seared his spine. He screamed and fought the hold of the whip.

And then a booted foot was on his chest.

John's gaze shot up to see Awai decked out in a leather catsuit, a whip curled in her hand, and she was staring down at him with a smirk on her face.

"You fucking bitch!" he shouted. He started to grab

her ankle when the low rumble of a jungle beast caused him to freeze.

Awai moved her foot as an enormous white-and-black striped tiger rose up within John's line of sight, and he was paralyzed with fear.

His body trembled and he tried to scramble away but the tiger pinned him to the floor with one massive paw against his chest.

"Still enjoy beating up women?" Awai asked in a deadly cold voice.

"Get your fucking pet off me," John said in a half-terrified, half-vicious tone.

"I don't think so." Awai squatted down beside him and smiled. "You won't be hurting any woman, ever again. Not ever, *slave*."

The tiger roared and John wet his pants, warm piss soaking his trousers. John screamed as the beast grabbed him by the collar and dragged him into the blinding white light.